RUBY STARR

THE FANTASTIC LIBRARY RESCUE

AND OTHER MAJOR PLOT TWISTS

Also by Deborah Lytton

Ruby Starr

RUBY STARR

THE FANTASTIC LIBRARY RESCUE

AND OTHER MAJOR PLOT TWISTS

DEBORAH LYTTON

Cover design by Jeanine Murch
Cover and internal illustrations by Jeanine Murch

Published by Sourcebooks Jabberwocky, an imprint of Sourcebooks, Inc.
P.O. Box 4410, Naperville, Illinois 60567-4410
(630) 961-3900
Fax: (630) 961-2168
sourcebooks.com

Library of Congress Cataloging-in-Publication Data

Names: Lytton, Deborah A., author. | Murch, Jeanine Henderson, illustrator.
Title: The fantastic library rescue and other major plot twists / Deborah Lytton ; cover and internal illustrations by Jeanine Murch.
Description: Naperville, Illinois : Sourcebooks Jabberwocky, [2018] | Series: Ruby Starr ; 2 | Summary: Members of Ruby Starr's lunchtime book club, the Unicorns, and other school book clubs come together to help when they learn that the school library is in financial trouble.
Identifiers: LCCN 2017037473 | (13 : alk. paper)
Subjects: | CYAC: Books and reading--Fiction. | Clubs--Fiction. | Friendship--Fiction. | Fund raising--Fiction. | Schools--Fiction. | Imagination--Fiction.
Classification: LCC PZ7.L9959 Fan 2018 | DDC [Fic]--dc23 LC record available at https://lccn.loc.gov/2017037473

Source of Production: Berryville Graphics, Berryville, Virgina, USA
Date of Production: March 2018
Run Number: 5011855

Printed and bound in the United States of America.
BVG 10 9 8 7 6 5 4 3 2 1

For Dad

I love you

CHAPTER 1

A New Beginning

Once upon a time, there lived a girl named Ruby Starr. (That's me.) If we haven't met before, I'd like to tell you some super-important things about me. If we *have* met before, you probably know most of this, but there are a few surprises.

1. I love, love, love books (even non-fiction books, especially ones about baking cakes)!
2. Chocolate can make even the worst day a little bit better. Trust me. I know this from personal experience.
3. My favorite color is the color of

dragons, pickles, and my eyes. Have you figured it out yet?

4. I have four besties—Siri, Jessica, Daisy, and Charlotte. Charlotte wasn't an instant bestie, but that's a whole other story!
5. Sometimes I imagine I am in the pages of a book. My thoughts sort of fly up into bubble-gum bubbles full of ideas. Sometimes that also gets me into trouble with a lowercase *t*.
6. I believe a good book should always have a sequel.

Today starts out as just an ordinary Tuesday. Well, except that every Tuesday is sort of extra-ordinary on account of the Unicorn Book Club. My friends and I have a special group that meets every Tuesday at lunch to discuss a book we are all reading at the same time. (A lot of books begin with a regular kind of day to set the stage for a new adventure.)

So, I am sitting at the lunch table in our usual spot with the other Unicorns: Siri, Jessica, Daisy, and Charlotte. Pink is our signature color, so we all have something pink on today. The sleuth in me needs to be specific about every detail. (*Sleuth* is on my spelling list for this week. It means detective, like Nancy Drew.) So here are the details: I have pink laces in my green sneakers and a pink headband holding back my curly hair. Siri is wearing a pink skirt, and Daisy has on a pink T-shirt with her jeans. Jessica and Charlotte are both wearing pink sweatshirts.

"Has anyone finished reading *Little Women*?" I ask. This is the way we begin every meeting. I check to see if anyone is done with the book, because no one wants to hear about the ending of a book before they have read it.

"I finished last night," Siri says before she

pops a grape into her mouth. Siri has been my best friend since kindergarten, and someday when she's a famous fashion designer and I am a famous author, she's going to design all my clothes for book signings. I already have my signature planned. It's going to look like this:

Ruby Starr☆

"Me too," says Daisy as she hands me a graham cracker. The Unicorns share lunch on Tuesdays. I brought a big red-and-white cloth napkin and spread it on the table where we all put our food. It feels more special that way, unless the boys at the other end of the table decide to have a food fight. Last time that happened, we ended up with orange peels in our veggie dip. No one wanted to eat anything after that.

"Ruby and I finished the book on Saturday," Charlotte adds with a grin at me. Her smiles are extra sparkly because of her pink braces. I grin back. Charlotte and I are reading buddies.

"I read the last page at breakfast this morning," Jessica shares. "I almost dropped the book in my cereal bowl." Everyone laughs. Only I laugh the most because I've almost dropped books in cereal, spaghetti, and even my dog Abe's water bowl (which usually has dog drool floating on the surface). I guess that's just what happens when you have a book with you at all times.

"We're all done. That is most excellent," I tell them in my fake British accent. Talking in a fake British accent is kind of my thing. I use it when I want to sound extra smart and wizardly.

I am already prepared with a question to get the group talking about the book. "Which one of the March sisters is your favorite and why?" I ask. Jo is my favorite of the four sisters because she is a writer, and also because my middle name is Josephine. But I don't say my answer out loud yet.

Since I asked the question, I think it's a good idea to let someone else answer first.

Jessica jumps in right away. "Beth for sure. Because she is the one who keeps the sisters tied together."

"Beth is the kindest one," Charlotte adds. "But I like Amy because she changes the most. She only thinks about herself at the beginning."

Siri hands each of us a strawberry. Then she says, "I like Jo because she's the strongest of the sisters."

"And she's a writer," I mumble as I bite into the berry.

Daisy shrugs and sighs. "Since you have all picked my favorites, I have to say Meg. Otherwise, she'll be completely left out."

Then Jessica asks if we liked the ending. But before we can answer, my friend Charissa and her two besties, Sophie and Brooke, come over to sit with us. We all smush closer together to make room.

"Did you choose your next book yet?" Charissa asks. Her book club is called the Macarons. (Fun fact: macarons are little French cookies that come in pretty colors like pink and lavender and even green!) One time, the Unicorns and Macarons joined up to read a book together. My mom says you can never have too many readers in a book club.

"Not yet," Daisy tells her. "Do you want to read the next one with us?"

We all agree that the Unicorns and the Macarons will be a team for the next book.

Which is why Charlotte says, "What should we read?"

Choosing a book is the most exciting part of being in a book club. There are so many choices. Suddenly, everyone is talking at once. I hear lots of titles I recognize, most of which I have already read. Suddenly, I am no longer at the lunch table. I am inside my imagination.

I find myself in a room filled with books. The walls are made of books, the stairs are made of books, and even the ceiling is made of books. I can't figure out which one to read! I choose the first book my hand touches. Only when I open the cover, a little bookworm pops his head out of the pages. He wears glasses and a top hat. The bookworm tells me if I can read every book in this room, he will make me the Keeper of the Library. I'd love to be in charge of all these books. So I start reading right away.

"Ruby? Do you have an idea for our next book?"

Siri is asking me a question. It's sad to realize I am here at school, not in a magical library with a talking bookworm.

"I was thinking about another classic," I tell them. "Like *Anne of Green Gables*." I love the classics.

"Has anyone heard of *The Misfit Girls*?" Siri asks. "I saw it at the bookstore."

"I want to read that book too," Charissa answers.

"Is it the one with five pairs of sneakers on the cover?" Daisy asks.

"Yes," Siri responds. "It's so cool. You read the ending first and then the rest of the story in reverse."

"You never read an ending first. It's the first rule of reading," I blurt out before I can stop myself.

No one speaks for at least a full minute.

Maybe even two minutes, and that's a super-long time for complete silence at lunch with a group of girls. It's almost like I've dumped a giant bucket of freezing-cold water on everyone.

And I know why. It's because I just sounded like our teacher, Mrs. Sablinsky. That's not a good thing because:

1. She has absolutely no sense of humor.
2. She never—and I mean never—makes exceptions to her rules.
3. She would probably not invite a talking chipmunk to tea.

(I would absolutely invite a talking chipmunk to tea, wouldn't you?)

Even though I don't want to sound like a mini-Mrs. Sablinsky, reading an ending before you reach the end of a book is a book people no-no. It just isn't done.

"It might be fun to try something new." Jessica is the first one to break the silence.

Uh-oh. I've been here before. This is like one of those déjà vu moments where something feels familiar even though it hasn't ever happened before. Except in my case, it actually has happened. And me *not wanting to try something new* ended up causing a lot of friend drama. Even possibly some tears (mostly mine). One thing about me is that I make a lot of lowercase *m* mistakes, but I do learn from them. So right now, instead of arguing about the book, I smile really big at my friends and say, "If everyone wants to read *The Misfit Girls*, then let's read it."

Maybe it will be fun to read a book backward. Maybe.

Just then, a slice of half-bitten cheese lands on the table next to me. It is followed by pieces of corn-puff cereal.

EWWWWWWWWWWWWWWWWWWWWWW!

The Unicorns and Macarons jump to our feet. Everyone reaches for their lunch bags and begins cleaning up as fast as possible. I am just folding up Mom's cloth napkin when something hits my left hand. I am almost afraid to look. I don't want to look. But bravery means overcoming fear. So, I shift my eyes to see what has landed on the table next to me.

It can't be. But it is. A half-bitten, very slimy piece of salami. (Secret fact about me: I really and truly can't stand salami.)

In a situation like this, Nancy Drew would remain calm. She wouldn't run away screaming.

I am no longer me. I am a famous sleuth solving a mystery. I must discover who threw the piece of salami. My personal opinions about this form of lunch meat are not important. What is important is to find clues. I take a closer look at the salami. It has something shiny on it. Could it be mayonnaise? Could it be saliva? Whoever had this salami probably began with a sandwich, so my first step will be to find two empty pieces of bread with one medium-size bite missing. Just then, I hear someone calling my name.

"Ruby, step away from the salami!" Jessica orders as she pulls me away from the table.

OK, I am not a brilliant and stylish sleuth in the middle of an investigation. I am here at the lunch table and about to actually touch the half-bitten piece of salami next to my hand. Not good.

Wow, that was really close. I might never have used this hand again. And it's my writing hand, so it's super-important. "Thank you for saving me," I tell her. "I don't know what happened back there."

"Let's get you to the library," she tells me. "Books will bring you back to yourself."

I grin at my friend. For book people like us, seeing pages and pages of stories just waiting to be read can make us happy.

The school librarian, Mrs. Xia, keeps the library open at lunch in case students would like to read. I think it's a really smart idea because sometimes a person (I'm not naming names) might have a worser-than-worse kind of day with friends and might need a place to hide for a little while. A place where it's not embarrassing to be alone.

"Maybe we can get copies of *The Misfit Girls*," Charlotte says with a spin and a whoosh of her long dark hair. (Charlotte fact: She's a dancer, and she's going to get pointe shoes soon. Ruby fact: I am not a dancer. I will never be getting pointe shoes unless they are on a poster to hang on my bedroom wall.) We all follow the whirling Charlotte through the red door into the school library.

"Hi, girls," Mrs. Xia greets us. "What are you reading this week?"

"We just finished *Little Women*," I tell her with a smile. I know she will like this choice. She loves the classics too.

Sure enough, Mrs. Xia claps her hands together and gets a sparkle in her eyes. "Wonderful choice. That book was ahead of its time, you know." Then she winks at us. "What are you reading next?"

"We decided to read *The Misfit Girls*," Siri tells her.

Mrs. Xia crinkles her forehead. "I'm not sure I am familiar with that one. Let me look it up."

She sits down at the computer and begins typing. All eight of us line up in front of her desk in a row. After a moment, she looks at us. "I'm sorry, girls. But the library doesn't have copies of this book."

"Not even one?" I ask. "It's a really popular new book."

Mrs. Xia shakes her head slowly. "I'm afraid we have had some budget cuts in the library. Right now, we don't have the funds to purchase new books—or even replace old ones."

There is a quiet moment then, as all of us try to understand what she's saying. I trade a look with Siri, who trades a look with Jessica until the look goes all the way down the line. We understand. No new books. No *Misfit Girls*.

"Perhaps I can help you select another book to read," Mrs. Xia suggests.

But Charissa speaks up. "Thank you very much, but we already agreed and everything."

Mrs. Xia nods like she understands, but I see her mouth crumple. Mrs. Xia loves books and helping kids find something wonderful to read. I can tell she feels bad that she doesn't have *The Misfit Girls* here.

"It isn't going to be easy to get copies for all of us," Jessica begins. "Maybe we should try to find something here with doubles at least."

"We didn't have this problem before," Brooke says.

"Because we were reading a classic," I remind her. We read *A Wrinkle in Time*—a super-great book club choice, I might add—and Charissa's teacher loaned us books from her classroom.

When the Unicorns choose a book, it's not so hard to find copies. We go to the school library or the local library or the bookstore. If we're reading a classic, I might have it at home already because my mom has a whole shelf of her favorite books from when she was my age. My brothers have a lot of books too. Once or twice, the Unicorns have even shared one copy of a book by reading it and then passing it around the group. And Jessica just got an e-reader for her birthday so now she can download books. (Fun fact: I've already put "e-reader" in the number one spot on my Christmas wish list.)

Here's the thing though. Combining the Unicorns and the Macarons means eight readers. And that makes finding copies way more complicated, especially since we chose a brand-new book.

That's when I have an idea to fix the problem. It just pops right into my head like a light bulb has turned on. Hey, I guess that poster on Mrs. Sablinsky's wall of the boy thinking with a light bulb over his head isn't just a cartoon. It's real life! (This is when the ordinary day becomes an adventure as the main character sets out on a difficult journey.)

"I'll try the local library after school. Maybe I can get copies for us." OK, so maybe going to the library isn't exactly a *difficult journey*. A girl can dream, can't she?

"Ruby is our hero!" Charlotte calls out. The other girls join in, chanting my name. "Ruby! Ruby!"

I'm really enjoying this hero moment...

I imagine myself as the superhero of books. I disguise myself as a librarian, but if there is a reader in need, I become Book Girl! I wear magical glasses that can spot books anywhere and have a book bag that looks ordinary on the outside but can actually hold hundreds of books on the inside. With my magical powers, I can climb the tallest bookcase, find an out-of-print book, speed-read faster than anyone in the world, and deliver copies of books to everyone who wants to read one!

I am saving the day until Mrs. Xia shushes us.

"Girls, this is still a library." She holds her finger to her lips. *Shhhhhhhhhhhh.*

And that's the end of my hero moment. But not the end of my journey.

CHAPTER 2

Journey to a Faraway Land (But Not Yet)

I'm still imagining myself walking into school with eight copies of *The Misfit Girls* when Mrs. Sablinsky begins introducing a new assignment. It isn't until she says the word *creative* that I wake up from my daydream. *Creative* is one of my favorite words, along with *imagination*, *llama*, and *squiggle*. The list keeps growing. I must have over twenty favorites now. Abe's favorite word is *cookie*. He doesn't get real cookies, just dog-safe treats that are made in the shape of a cookie, which I am pretty sure is done more for the dog owner than the dog. Abe would eat the treat no matter what it looks like.

I listen to Mrs. Sablinsky. "This is a creative

writing assignment. Every student is to write a poem by Friday. The format and subject are up to you. If you would like to read your poem out loud at our first Fifth Grade Poetry Read, please let me know when you turn in your work."

There is a lot of excitement in the room about the first Poetry Read. We all want to be part of a new tradition. It's like the entire class begins talking at once.

Mrs. Sablinsky rings the little bell on her desk to get our attention. Everyone quiets down. "That's better. Now, may I please have a volunteer to read the first poem on page seventeen of your textbook?"

I raise my hand, but she doesn't choose me. Truth: Mrs. Sablinsky almost never calls on me, even when I am being quiet and raising my hand nicely. I'm not really surprised when she chooses Will P instead since he's her absolute favorite student. There are two Wills in our class, so we have to use their last name initials to tell them apart. Not that they look the same or anything. Will P is supersmart and makes up completely amazing words like *fantastical* and wears red glasses. Plus, he's my friend. Will B picks his nose a lot (I mean *a lot*). I won't even share the rest of what he does. He is an OK artist though. Mom says everyone has something to like about them. I guess that's true even for a boy who picks his nose for fun.

Will P reads the poem about walking through a busy city.

Then Mrs. Sablinsky asks for some observations about the poem. After that, she introduces the next poem in the book. "This poem is called a haiku. It is a type of poetry that originated in Japan. Most haikus are written about nature. So, if you are going to write about nature, you might consider using this format. There are only three lines in the poem. The first line is five syllables, the second line is seven syllables, and the third line is five syllables."

I like nature. I raise my hand to read the poem out loud. Guess what? Mrs. Sablinsky doesn't choose me. Instead, she chooses Siri. The haiku is about the sea, and the words make me feel like I am looking at the ocean. No, wait, like I'm *in* the ocean.

I see the ocean rolling up and down with the words of the haiku dancing on the tops of the waves. I ride my surfboard across the water and catch each word. An otter wearing sunglasses floats past me with the word *sea* in her paws. A sea turtle carries the word *waves* on his shell. Then a blue whale spouts *sapphire*. After I gather all the words, I make my own poem.

How the sea glistens
With waves of pearl and sapphire,
Calling out to me.

Suddenly, Mrs. Sablinsky glides by on a stand-up paddleboard and says, "Everyone please get started on your assignments now." The words of poetry drift apart and are pulled away by the current.

I take out a blank piece of paper and my favorite green pencil. I think I want to write a long rhyming poem. I like to rhyme words: *Fun* and *sun*. *Hi* and *bye*. I'm a mine of rhymes (ha!) except that I'm not really sure what to write about. I look around the room for inspiration. Good writers observe the world around them to use in their writing.

Mrs. S loves cats so she has lots of cat-related items in Room 15. A cat on one poster wears a pair of bunny ears. Another poster has a list of transitional words made out of paw prints. Cat mugs sit in a line on Mrs. Sablinsky's desk, and underneath it there is even a waste paper basket in the shape of... Can you guess it? A cat! So unless I want to write a poem about cats, I don't think the scenery is going to spark any ideas. Besides, I'm one hundred percent a dog person.

Then I notice something on the wall near my desk. We recently switched seats, and I'm in the front of the room now, which would be great except that all my friends are in the back of the room. Also, I'm sitting next to Jason, the kid who sleeps during class and drools all over his books. (Note that I am not sitting at the danger zone that is Desk One for two reasons:

1. Will B used to sit there.
2. He used the underside of his desk as a tissue.)

Getting back to my point, sometimes when you change seats in a classroom, you notice things you never noticed before—like a calendar on the side board that says *November* at the top decorated with brown and gold leaves.

November. That's a pretty good theme for a poem. I decide to go with it.

November, how your leaves inspire me

In gold and brown and red

Hey, this is almost professional!

Like a wreath a princess wears on her head

What does that have to do with November? OK, maybe not so professional after all. I'm sure if Mrs. Sablinsky read these words, she'd sigh, like she always does when she deals with me.

Siri comes over to my desk.

"How's it going, Ruby?"

I wrinkle my nose. "I only have two good lines so far. What about you?"

Siri holds up her paper. And I can't believe my eyes—it's completely filled with writing. "I love poetry!" she tells me with a bright smile. "I wrote about the Statue of Liberty."

Oh, that's really smart. We've been learning a

lot about Lady Liberty, as Mrs. Sablinsky likes to call her. Big words like *liberty* and *freedom* would sound good in a poem. But I can't write one on the same subject. It would be like stealing Siri's idea. Plus, I'm Ruby Starr—I'm the Queen of Imagination. I can come up with my own creative and brilliant idea. So, I crumple the princess with the crown of leaves and start over.

I take out a new piece of paper and put my name on the top. Except when the bell rings, that's still the only thing on the page.

"Leave your work in your desk folders," Mrs. Sablinsky tells us. "This is an in-class project only."

In other words, she doesn't want our parents writing the poems for us. On the last project we had on biomes, Jason's mom went crazy and planted real grass and little trees in a cardboard box. Then she created animals out of thread and pebbles. It was like something you would see in a museum. Mrs. S was not impressed. She got that pinched expression like she smelled stinky cheese and said, "This will not do, not at all."

Since then, all our projects have been in-class projects. (Fun fact: Biomes are areas with the same weather, animals, and plants, like deserts, grasslands, and forests. I like the savannah best because lions live there. Lions are very literary animals. I mean, they live in Oz and Narnia, two of my favorite book places.)

I hurry out to the front of school with the other Unicorns. I can't wait to get to the library.

"Good luck," Siri says with a wide grin.

"Fingers crossed," Charlotte adds.

I give them one of my signature winks. I close my right eye and nod at the same time. I've practiced in the mirror to get them just right. Believe me, it takes a *lot* of practice. This is my way of saying that they can count on me.

In the crowd of parents and kids, I spot my

grandma right away. She's wearing black-and-white-checked golf shorts with a blue shirt.

"Hi, sweetie pie," she says as I hurry over for a hug. "How was your day?"

Today my grandma is picking me up from school because it's Tuesday and my mom usually works late on Tuesdays. So, Gram picks me and my brothers, Sam and Connor, up from school. Only Sam and Connor go to different schools and get out later than I do, so there's usually time for an ice cream or a trip to the library for a super-important mission.

"Pretty OK," I tell her. "I really need to go to the library. Would you take me?"

Gram slings my backpack over her shoulder and slips her arm around my shoulders. "It would be my pleasure."

When we get to the parking lot, I find Gram's car right away. It's just an ordinary white SUV. Except my grandma dresses her car for every season. Since we are close to Thanksgiving, she has red, yellow, and orange turkey feathers fanning across the roof of the car. A pair of eyelashes is on the front headlights so they look like eyes. Also, her license plate says, GRAMBUS. You really can't miss it.

"I need to get eight copies of a book for the Unicorns," I tell Gram. "They're counting on me."

She winks as she opens the door for me. "Then we better hurry."

I climb into the backseat and belt in so my hero's journey can begin. I know, I know. I am fully aware that going in Grambus to the local library isn't like jumping on a magic carpet and flying off to Neverland. But when I open the pages of any one of the gazillion books on the shelves, I do journey to another place.

My magic carpet is actually an open book. I sit in the middle of the pages with my sidekicks, a hedgehog named Dot and a ladybug named Spike. We fly over lands from all the stories I have read. There is a castle with a bear king, an island of mermaids, a miniature city of talking mice, a creaky old house with a crooked tree, an open plain filled with wild horses, and even a giant beanstalk leading to a kingdom of golden birds. My imagination can take me anyplace I want to go.

"Ruby, we're here." My grandma's voice lands my book carpet ride in the parking lot of the library.

"That was fast," I say as we get out of the car. The doors of the library open automatically for us like we are famous. (Except I am pretty sure the doors do that for everyone.)

I hurry to the children's section of the library. I don't have to worry about Gram keeping up. She's a super-sporty kind of grandma. Plus, she wears magic sneakers. PS: They aren't really magic like Dorothy's slippers. She just says they help her keep up with me.

I am happy to see that my favorite librarian, Miss Mary, is here today. I rush over to explain the situation.

"Hi, Miss Mary. I am on a super-important mission to locate eight copies of *The Misfit Girls* right away."

"Hi yourself, Miss Ruby. Is this a top-secret spy mission?" Miss Mary asks with a grin.

"Not top secret," I confide. "But important because I need them ASAP." (I've heard my dad say ASAP sometimes on the phone about work. It's a shortcut for *as soon as possible*.)

Miss Mary nods. "*The Misfit Girls* is a really popular book. I know we have a number of copies. I'm not sure about eight though."

"Even six would work," I try. Charlotte and I can share since we're reading book club books together. And Jessica reads so fast that she could hand it off to Daisy in one day probably.

"I'll see what I can do," Miss Mary says.

Gram takes a seat on the blue-and-yellow-striped sofa. I look around at all the books on the shelves. So many adventures are waiting inside the covers. It makes me happy just thinking about all the books there that I haven't read yet.

"What else happened at school today?" Gram says as I sit down beside her. She tugs on one of my curls.

"We're writing poetry. And we're going to invite people to come and hear us read our poems out loud. Would you and Grandpa come?"

Gram hugs me. "We wouldn't miss it!"

That's the good thing about family. You always have a cheering section.

"You're already a poet. You wrote that wonderful poem about Abe and George for Grandpa's birthday," Gram says with a chuckle. My dog, Abe, is the brother of my grandparents' dog, George. Things to know about Abe and George:

1. They are Labradoodles (half Labrador retriever and half poodle).
2. They are named after presidents. (Can you guess which ones? Hint: #1 and #16.)
3. They get into a lot of mischief, especially when they are together.

Gram is right, I did write a pretty good poem for my grandpa's birthday. But I don't think I would want to read it out loud in front of the whole school. No, my class poem needs to be way more impressive. It needs to be fabulously fabulous.

Just then, Miss Mary returns with a book in her hands. Wait—a book. One book! Seven less than I need!

"I'm sorry, Ruby, but it appears all the other copies are checked out. I do have one copy though." She holds the book out for me. I see the five pairs of sneakers on the cover. "I can put your name on a waiting list for the other copies."

I sigh. I have failed in my mission. Seven people were counting on me, and I have let them down. That's all I'm thinking as I thank Miss Mary and tell her that there is no need to put my name on a list. I can't wait a week or even a few days. My mission has a one-day deadline.

"Shall we check it out?" Gram asks as she

takes the book from Miss Mary. "One is better than none."

I study the black-and-white checks on Grandma's shorts. They look like a chessboard without the pieces. Somehow, that makes me sad, as if the pieces are all lost. My brothers and I have a game cabinet with all these board games in it. A few of the puzzles are missing pieces. When you have spent over an hour fitting one thousand teeny-tiny pieces together to make Winnie the Pooh and his friends (OK, some of the puzzles have been in that cabinet for a really long time!), and then Piglet is missing an eye, it kind of takes the excitement out of finishing the puzzle.

I shrug and answer Gram, "Maybe if there were three of us, but eight girls can't read one book. Not in time for the next meeting anyway."

Gram gives the book back to the librarian at the counter. I don't see Miss Mary to say good-bye so I follow my grandma out the door. I've never left the library without a book before. This is a first for me. A first I would rather not repeat.

The Southern California sunshine can sometimes turn a sour mood into a cheery one. Not today. I didn't even want to read this book in the first place, but I promised the Unicorns I would save the day.

Superheroes
don't
fail
in
their
missions.

They always succeed.

That's when I remember: the library isn't the only place to get a book.

Of course! I don't know why I didn't think of this right away. The bookstore is my favorite place to get a present. (In case you are ever stumped about what to get me: books, book marks, book lights—you get the idea. Anything that begins with the letters: *b-o-o-k.*) I know this sounds completely weird, but confession time: I love, absolutely love the way a new book smells.

Every good hero faces obstacles and has to come up with a Plan B, right? So here goes my Plan B:

"I bet the bookstore has eight copies of *The Misfit Girls*. Could you take me there?" I ask Gram as I climb into the backseat.

"I'm sorry, sweetie pie, but we're out of time. We have to go pick up your brothers now."

The bookstore that used to be in my neighborhood closed, and the second-nearest bookstore isn't really that near at all. So much for Plan B. And now I'm all out of ideas.

"Maybe your friends can each try to get a copy of the book," Gram suggests. "Buying eight books is a tall order, even for a grandma who likes to spoil her best granddaughter."

I grin a little at Gram's joke. I am her only granddaughter. And I know buying eight copies of a book would cost a lot.

"You're right," I agree. Of course everyone could go out and find the book themselves. That's the way it usually works. Except that someone wanted to be a hero (or in my case, a superhero) and save the day.

"Maybe you could choose another book?" Gram suggests as she pulls into the pickup line at Connor's school.

"I would, but it's not that easy to get eight fifth graders to agree."

"I believe there are at least that many members in your mother's book club. How do they agree on a book to read?" Gram asks as she hands me a granola bar.

My mom's book club is what inspired me to

start my own. I have been to all of her meetings except for one (but that is a whole other story) so I have heard them choose books before. "Mom asks everyone to suggest a book. Then she makes a list and has them vote on which one to read first. They go through the list week by week."

"That is what leadership is all about," Gram tells me. "And you, my dear girl, are a born leader."

Yum, the granola bar has chocolate chips in it. Remember number two on the list of super-important things about me? Well, chocolate really does make things better. And that must be why by the time Connor gets into the car, I have come up with a Plan C.

CHAPTER 3

Plan C or Possibly Plan D

Dinner at the Starr house is the opposite of simple because every person in my family eats a different way. Except for me. I eat everything.

So Burger Night here isn't traditional. Our choices for this evening are veggie burgers, lettuce wraps for the no-bread customers, and double beef burgers for the serious meat eater. (That would be my brother Sam.) There is also a platter of french fries. My favorite thing though is the bowl of pickles. I'd eat a plate of pickles if Mom would let me. She wouldn't.

Sam and Connor and I are sitting in our usual chairs. Abe has assumed his favorite mealtime position right underneath the table. That's in case anyone drops something scrumptious.

Sam and Connor are only two years apart, but they couldn't be more different. The best way to explain it is this: if Sam had to choose something to take with him to a deserted island, he would choose a basketball. And Connor would choose a microscope. I bet you can guess what I would choose. Hint: it begins with a *B*. Mom is just setting the salad on the table when Abe starts whimpering and runs to the door. Then he sits there wagging his tail.

I know what that means. "Dad's home," I announce.

The door opens, and voilà, there is my dad. Abe starts jumping up on him like he's been gone for weeks, but he's only been at work since breakfast time. Grandpa told me once that dogs don't understand time the way we do. So maybe Abe thinks hours are days or months even.

"*Bonsoir, ma famille*," Dad says as he comes through the door. He's studying French, and he practices on us. I'm starting to learn what some of the words mean. I'm pretty sure "*Bonsoir, ma famille*" means "Good evening, my family."

"You're just in time," Mom says with a smile.

I run over and give him a hug. Dad drops a kiss on my head. "How was your book club today?"

"Good until the boys started their food fight at the other end. I actually got hit with a half-eaten piece of salami." I scrunch my face at the memory.

"*Très désagréable*," Dad says as he hugs me again. Then he heads to the sink to wash his hands.

"Translation, please?" Connor asks.

"Very unpleasant," Dad calls over his shoulder.

I hurry back to the table. Mom is serving the salad. It's a rainbow of veggies with yellow bell peppers, red cherry tomatoes, shredded carrots, sliced celery, cucumber, and dark-green lettuce. Sam chopped them all up like the chefs on television. For a fifteen-year-old, he's pretty impressive in the kitchen. I helped peel the carrots, and I have to say that they are especially delicious tonight.

"I'm starving," Sam says as he makes a double burger for himself.

"We know," Connor answers. Everyone laughs at that because Sam is always hungry.

Sometimes after his football games, he eats an entire carton of eggs and drinks a whole quart of milk!

I choose a veggie burger and pile it with seven pickles. Then I stack few extras on the side of my plate, just in case.

"Have I mentioned that I love pickles?" I tell my family.

"We know," Connor answers again. Everyone laughs because of course my family already knows this. They know everything about me.

Mom laughs the most because every time we

are at the grocery store, I add a jar of pickles to the shopping cart. I love Mom's laugh. She has the kind of laugh that makes anyone who hears it smile. It isn't one of those funny laughs that are super-squeaky or booming. It's a rainbow-across-a-cloudy-sky laugh.

I imagine skateboarding on the rainbow of Mom's laugh. My skateboard is gold with green wheels that flash pink when they spin. I jump on my board at the giant bend on the top of the rainbow and zigzag across red to jump over orange and land on yellow. Then I slide over to green. My brothers and my dad are riding their own skateboards. We're all gliding along until Abe whooshes past us on a dog-size skateboard. We hurry to catch up. The end of the rainbow is a garden made entirely of books.

Dad says, "Ruby, what are you reading for your next book club?"

Hey, wait a second. I'm not in a garden of books. I'm still at the dinner table with my family, and Abe is still making the most out of his spot underneath the table.

I look around to see everyone waiting on my answer. "Well, I don't exactly know yet," I say. And with a deep breath, I tell my family the whole story about the search for *The Misfit Girls*.

My story ends with: "So now I have to go to school tomorrow and tell the Unicorns and the Macarons that I don't have the books."

"Your friends will understand," Connor offers.

"It's not your fault," Sam adds. "You tried your best."

That's one of the Starr Family Rules: Always try your best.

Mom and Dad aren't like some parents who expect straight A's all the time. (Only Connor gets

A's all the time anyway.) They tell me and Sam and Connor to do our best no matter what. As long as we have given something our full attention and best effort, they are proud of us.

"At first, I thought maybe we could go to the bookstore," I admit. "But then I realized that buying eight copies of a book would be kind of expensive. Gram helped me figure that out. Plus, I didn't even really want to read it, so I don't think it would be right to ask you to buy it for everyone in the group. So I came up with a Plan C."

"Plan C?" Dad asks as he hands me the ketchup.

"To have a meeting and choose another book." I make a star shape on the side of my plate and then dip a french fry into the star. Yum.

"Have you ever noticed when my book club chooses the next book?" Mom asks as she fills my water glass.

It's not polite to speak when your mouth is full, so I shake my head no.

"We don't wait until we finish discussing a book. We choose when we are one or two meetings away from finishing. That way, we all have time to get the next book."

Oh. Well, that makes sense. Except that we didn't exactly plan this reading together thing. It just sort of happened.

"I do the same thing at work," Dad says with a grin. He and Connor have matching smiles. "I choose the new story before I finish the current story. So we don't lose time figuring out what to do next."

Dad is a writer for the local morning news. His pieces are always about ordinary people doing interesting things in our community. Someday I'm going to be a writer too. Only I am going to write books for readers like me. I'll be Ruby J. Starr, author extraordinaire.

"That's how it is with chess," Connor adds. "I am always thinking at least two moves ahead. How do you think I beat Sam every time?"

"Hey!" Sam argues. "Not every time."

"Admit it. I win every time," Connor teases. "I'm just that good."

He's right. No one can beat Connor at chess. Not even Dad.

"I challenge you to a match after dinner." Sam doesn't give up easily.

"Challenge accepted." Connor winks at me. I grin back. I'm looking forward to watching them play. Maybe I can even play a game with the winner (who will probably be Connor).

After that, we take turns telling more stories about our days until all the french fries are gone and the pickle bowl has made its way around the table to me again.

The next morning, when I arrive at school, Siri runs up to me first. Her hair is braided in two fishtail braids. Fishtail braids are supercool and easy to do. Here's a quick lesson:

1. Put the hair into two ponytails.
2. Split one ponytail into two sides.
3. Bring one small piece of hair across from one side to the other. Hold tight.
4. Reverse and bring one small piece of hair from the other side back to the first side.
5. Keep going back and forth until the ponytail is finished. Secure with a hair elastic.
6. Do the other ponytail the same way.
7. Ta-da! That's the fishtail braid.

I imagine myself and Siri as mermaids sitting in seashell chairs at the underwater hair salon. Little butterfly fish are braiding our hair. They swim back and forth and back and forth. Next to us, a crab is having her claws painted hot pink by an octopus, and a manta ray is getting her makeup done by the very same octopus. He does have eight arms after all. Siri hugs me and asks: "Did you get the books from the library?"

Hold on, I'm not a mermaid. I'm here at school. And whether I like it or not, I have to admit to my friend that I failed.

Correction: *friends*. Because by then, Jessica, Daisy, and Charlotte are also there. I shake my head.

"The library only had one copy. We can put our names on a waiting list, but I have no idea how long it will take to get enough copies."

I expect to see disappointment on the Unicorn's faces. What I don't expect is this:

Daisy hugs me.

Jessica shrugs and says, "Thanks for trying anyway."

Siri throws an arm around my shoulders. "You're still our hero."

Charlotte nods. "We can pick another book."

That's the amazing thing about best friends. They like you no matter what.

I think this day can't get any better.

Only it does. Because when we arrive in the classroom, Mrs. Sablinsky tells us that the fifth-grade teachers have a meeting at the district office. Since we don't have substitutes, all fifth graders are going to the library. Can you believe it?

So that's how the Unicorns and the Macarons have a mini book club meeting on a Wednesday. We sit together at one of the back tables and talk about books. It's a dream day, really and truly.

I take notes on the ideas. The trouble is that out of eight girls, there isn't one match. We all suggest different titles. Here are my notes:

- Ruby: *Robin Hood*
- Jessica: *The Clue in the Diary* (Nancy Drew, Book 7)
- Siri: Any Harry Potter (but not the first one)
- Charissa: Something brand new
- Daisy: A horse story

- Brooke: Any book that isn't more than 150 pages
- Sophie: A young adult book like *Twilight*

I hold up the list dramatically like I am announcing the winner of an Academy Award for best actress. Except there is no winner.

"Since we all have different ideas, we're going to have to decide which of these books to read first. Then each week we can read another one on the list until everyone has had their chance. The only problem is that my mom doesn't let me read young adult books." I look over at Sophie. "Do you want to make another choice?"

Here's the thing. I know a few girls in my grade who have older sisters. They talk about young adult books. I asked Mom about it once, and she told me I can read young adult books when I am twelve or thirteen. That's almost two years from now. (Important fact about me: My birthday is August 3. I'm a Leo.)

"I can't read young adult books either," Jessica admits.

Charlotte pipes up. "My grandmother would not be happy about it. At all."

Sophie shrugs. "Then make my choice the same as Brooke's. Not more than 150 pages."

I look over the list again. I know my friends have been really supportive about the failed library mission, but I can't stop thinking about it. That's when I get an idea. It's funny how something going wrong can help something else go right.

"I just realized something." All seven girls turn to look at me at once. "Maybe we should look for all of these books and choose whichever one has extra copies."

If we agree on a book and then can't find it again, we'll be back to the same problem: no book club book to read. This way, we will have a book for sure.

We split into groups of two. Each team looks for both of their titles. I am paired with Jessica, and we decide to try for her book first. Mrs. Xia keeps the fiction shelves organized in alphabetical order beginning with the first letter of the author's last name. We're searching for Keene, Carolyn.

"My dad told me that Carolyn Keene is actually a pseudonym," I share with Jessica. "The real author of the Nancy Drew mysteries was a ghostwriter named Mildred Wirt Benson." I love interesting book facts.

Jessica grins at me. "Wow, that's like a mystery all on its own."

We are at the K's when we run into Will P and his friend Bryden. One thing to know about Will P: he has a signature sock collection that is school famous. Because of that, he lives in shorts year-round so that his socks are always on display.

(I'm serious. Even when it is raining out, Will P wears shorts.) Today, he is featuring gray socks with Mickey Mouse faces all over them.

"Hi, Ruby, are you looking for something for book club?" Will P asks as he pushes his red glasses higher on his nose. His brown hair swoops over the glasses and to the side.

"We're trying to find at least a few copies of a book that we all want to read. We're combining two groups this time so there are eight of us."

Will P's blue eyes get wide behind his glasses. "And I thought it was hard to find four copies." Will P is in a book club called the Polar Bears. Sometimes I read books with them.

Bryden rolls his eyes. "The library only has old books anyway."

Bryden is not one of my favorite people since he's usually the number one food fighter. But I have to agree with him.

"I think it's sort of a secret, but Mrs. Xia said

they have had some budget cuts. She can't buy any new books right now," I explain. I spot the Nancy Drew novels. I don't have to look for Keene. I can find them by the bright-yellow spines. "There they are." I point them out to Jessica. "On the next-to-bottom row."

Jessica and I look over the titles. Book seven is there.

"Only one copy," she says quietly. I would have liked to read this book as a group (even though I have already read it twice).

"Let's try *Robin Hood* now," she suggests.

Will P and Bryden are still standing there. They look a bit clueless, if you ask me. I, however, am a library expert. I'm what you might call a junior librarian because sometimes I help Mrs. Xia reshelve books.

"What book are you looking for?" I ask in my junior librarian voice, which is really no different from my regular voice.

Will P grins at me. "We wanted to read the new Kingdom Keepers." I know that series. I haven't read it yet, but it's on my wish list. Will P's book selections are always good ones. "Except the library doesn't have it. So we're doing the same thing. Looking for something with four copies."

"I'm sorry we are so limited," Mrs. Xia says as she overhears us talking. "It may be awhile before we can purchase new titles or extra copies to help those of you with book clubs. I hope it doesn't discourage you from reading as a group."

"It won't," I assure her. Will says the same thing. Only I wonder if he's thinking what I am thinking: how long can we keep our book clubs together if it's so hard to find books? The thought hurts my heart.

CHAPTER 4

A Poet I Am Not

Mrs. Sablinsky is back before lunch. She gives us a pop quiz on the poems we read in class yesterday. (Since I was listening, this is easy-peasy, lemon-squeezy.) When we finish, we can work on a word search until the bell rings. I look through the box on the back table to find one I haven't done before. Magic hat, check. Flower, check. Rainbow, check. I guess I could do the rainbow one again. Wait, here's one I haven't seen before. It's the American flag.

Guess what? I find all the words. (Hint: there are ten terms to find.)

Freedom
Colonies
Independence
Patriot
Founding Fathers
Nation
Liberty
Constitution
Revolution
Brave

Q F F R E E D O M L R L J J Y
C E O M H N C O L O N I E S A
K O U K M Z O D J C G E I Y W
H I N D E P E N D E N C E P R
W L D S W R M R D U A G Q Z X
C P I W T K E L W G T L T S G
K U N W D I H V Q P I I L S I
A X G I E R T J O M O B G N D
C A F D S P A U L L N E I P I
A H A S M J M U T L U R A M E
N O T L U P A T R I O T S Z Q
Z M H S G J M N Q I O Y I X Y
J S E H B R A V E N A N U O G
H T R Y L Z L F F V V H A G N
P C S P F O M K U M T J A Y P

At lunch, my friends and I share our clues from the library search. (OK, I know it's not really a mystery, but every story needs a little sleuthing.) I update my list just to keep track. So far, here is what we know about available books:

- Ruby: *Robin Hood*—two copies but different versions of the story
- Jessica: *The Clue in the Diary* (Nancy Drew, Book 7)—only one copy
- Siri: Any Harry Potter (but not the first one)—three copies of Book 1, two copies of Book 3
- Charissa: Something brand new—none
- Daisy: A horse story—only picture books and nonfiction books available
- Brooke: Any book that isn't more than 150 pages—nothing with eight copies

- Sophie: ~~A young adult book like *Twilight*~~ Any book that isn't more than 150 pages—nothing with eight copies

"Our best choice would be Harry Potter, Book Three," I tell the group. "We would be starting with two copies."

"I haven't read Book Two yet," Daisy says. "I kinda don't want to skip."

"Same here," agrees Charissa.

It's true that the best way to read a series is in order. But even though I understand Daisy and Charissa not wanting to read Book Three, that leaves us with exactly zero options. I munch on a carrot and try to come up with a Plan D. There has to be something we can all read.

I am on my way to a magical city of books where I can find as many copies as I wish. Only first I have to cross the Bridge of Courage. It is made of tiny planks of wood held together by golden vines. I step onto the first plank, and it moves underneath my feet. Below, I can see a deep canyon with no end. "Who goes there?" calls out a big, booming voice. It is the Troll of the Bridge of Courage. He is hidden underneath the bridge. Even though I can't see him, I can hear him. "You must pay for your crossing with a poem," he tells me. "Do you have one?" I don't have a poem. Not yet, anyway. I sit down crisscross applesauce to think.

I am sitting crisscross applesauce on the lunch bench. But there isn't a troll in sight.

"We can try the library again," Daisy suggests.

"Maybe we can ask Mrs. Sablinsky," Charlotte offers. Charlotte just moved here last month, and she doesn't know Mrs. S as well as I know her. Also, I think Mrs. Sablinsky likes her. Not as much as she likes Will P, but more than she likes me. In my experience, when you think a teacher likes you, it makes you go to them for help, even for the non-school kind of help.

"You can ask her if you want," I respond. Mom always says it can't hurt to ask. I suppose that's true even here, even with Mrs. Sablinsky. Maybe she has eight copies of something that is on our list.

A bigger problem is bothering me though. I can't stop thinking about what Mrs. Xia said about the library. A library without new books would be like a world without sunshine. What if students stop going because there isn't anything new to read? Then Mrs. Xia would be all alone day after day. That's why I say, "Daisy's right. Let's go back to the library."

I want to ask Mrs. Xia more questions about the budget cuts. And how long they will last. But when we get to the library door, we see a sign that reads *New library hours: Monday, Wednesday, and Friday only.*

The budget cuts must be more serious than I thought. I hold the door open for everyone. My friends head for the shelves of fiction books. I hurry to the front desk where Mrs. Xia is repairing old books.

"I saw the sign on the door," I tell her. "Is that because of the budget cuts?" Mrs. Xia nods, and her mouth pinches on the sides like she is trying to keep her words in.

"I'm sorry," I say softly. Then I point to the

stack of damaged books. "Can I help?" I love repairing books. It's a way to give them new life so they can reach more readers.

"I can always use help from my favorite junior librarian," she says as she hands me the little bottle of special book glue.

I take the top book off the stack. When I open it, the spine and the pages come apart. I use the little brush in the bottle to smooth a thin layer of glue onto the spine. Then I press the pages into place and hold.

"What are you reading right now?" Mrs. Xia asks.

"That's sort of the trouble," I admit. "Nothing. Either we agree and can't find enough copies, or we can't agree at all." I don't want to make her feel worse about the library not having enough copies for our book club so I think of something else to say. "I probably should be reading poetry though." I sigh, remembering the blank page with only my name at the top. "We have this assignment where we have to write a poem. I come up with ideas and even write a few lines, but that's all."

"Ah." Mrs. Xia claps her hands together and gets that book-people twinkle in her eyes. "Poetry is the most creative of the writing forms. Have you read much of it?"

I shake my head. Other than the few poems we read in class, I haven't read much at all.

Mrs. Xia brushes the glue on a loose book page and slides it into place. I help with the single pages sometimes, and I am really careful to make sure the page numbers line up. No one wants to be on page 10 and then skip to page 35 just because the page was glued in the wrong spot.

Mrs. Xia sets the repaired book to the side. "I have a whole shelf of poetry. Would you like to see?"

She seems so happy that even though I am really enjoying gluing the books, I grin and say, "Absolutely."

Mrs. Xia takes me to the back of the library. I don't usually spend much time in this section because most of the books are word puzzle books and books about computer games, things like that. Mrs. Xia points to the very last shelf near the bottom. There are about ten books of different shapes and sizes on it.

"Maybe you will get some inspiration from these," she says as she hands me a small white book that says *Poems for Kids* in letters made out of flowers on the cover.

"Thank you," I say as I sit down in the small chair near the window. Then, "Can I ask you something?"

She smiles at me. "Of course, Ruby." I know she expects that my question will have something to do with books. And it does. Kind of.

"Is the district going to close the library?" This is my greatest fear. The one I have been afraid to even think about.

Mrs. Xia sits down beside me. "I shouldn't have told you about the budget cuts. It wasn't appropriate for me to speak of such things with students. But the library isn't closing. We're just going through some changes. That's all." She pats me on the shoulder. "I don't want you to worry. The library will always be here. And I'll do my best to repair every book so that we keep as many as possible on the shelves."

Mrs. Xia leaves me alone after that. I open the book of poems and read through the first few before the bell rings. One thing I notice is that they don't all rhyme. I also notice that nature is very popular. Some of them are even kind of funny.

Siri and the rest of my friends meet me on the way to class. No one is holding a book, so that's not a good sign.

Charissa crosses her arms and gives me the report. "Here's the thing. Unless we want to read a book of fairy tales, there isn't anything here with more than three copies. Nothing we agree on anyway."

I'd read a book of fairy tales, but I can tell from the expressions on everyone else's faces that this is a definite no. So we still don't have a book to read. And now our days at the school library are limited. All in all, not the best lunch ever.

When we return to the classroom, something really unusual happens. Mrs. Sablinsky actually puts me in a good mood. She reminds us that tomorrow is Pajama Day. So everyone can come to school in their pajamas! (I love Pajama Day because everyone acts like it's a giant sleepover even though we aren't eating popcorn and staying up all night. You know that feeling when you are at a sleepover and you really want to go to sleep but you don't want to be the first one? So you keep your eyes open even though they are as heavy as dictionaries. That's the worst part of a sleepover. The best part is everything else!)

After the exciting Pajama Day announcement, Mrs. Sablinsky tells us that we can have the rest of the day to work on our poetry assignments. *Yippee!* Mrs. S hands out our works in progress. (That's a writer term.) When she gets to me, her lips pinch closed and her eyebrows rise so high that they disappear underneath her hair.

"Ruby, this time is to write your poetry, not to daydream."

I nod. "I am working on it. I just started over, that's all."

Mrs. Sablinsky's eyebrows come back to their usual places. "Very well. As long as you're making progress. Remember, it has to be finished in class."

"I know," I say as I take the paper with my name on it. And nothing else.

Which is exactly how the paper looks when Charlotte comes over to see how it's going. Her poem is finished now too. She has written about books. Books? That's my thing. Why didn't I think of that?

She asks me to read her poem. I have to admit, it's really good. It rhymes and everything.

"It is most impressive," I tell her in my fake British accent. "I expect high marks for this poem." When I use my British accent, I like to throw in some fancier words than usual. Sometimes it's fun to try being someone else. Especially when the someone you are can't think of a single subject to write about!

"Thanks!" Charlotte says with a shy smile. I know reading hasn't always been her favorite subject, even though it is now. I also know I had something to do with it.

That's why I add in my regular Ruby voice, "Seriously, Charlotte. I wish I had written this." I do. I wish I had written anything!

After she leaves, I look over at my neighbor,

Jason. He's sleeping as usual. Wait a minute. He's filled an entire sheet of paper with writing! How in the world did he manage that without waking up?

I look around the room. Everyone is writing except for the students walking around. Mrs. S lets us share completed creative writing with our classmates to get feedback. So that means all the students walking around the room are finished. That's at least half the class. Even Will B is sharing his poem.

Arrrrrrrgggggghhhhhhh! I stare at the blank sheet.

Poetry. Poetry. I remember the examples I read at lunch. They were all about feelings. Thoughts. I write fiction stories that are all about adventure. I think of the poem I wrote for Grandpa's birthday. I could do something like that, I guess. But it wasn't a poemy kind of poem. It was a birthday card kind of poem.

I lean my arms on the desk and rest my chin on them. Maybe I could write about not being able to write.

Or maybe I could write about…

Mrs. Sablinsky cuts into my writer's block by saying, "Only poems submitted on time will be eligible for the Poetry Read."

Great. Just great. Now if I don't hurry up and write something, I won't even get to read out loud. Then Grandpa and Gram will be sitting in the audience, and I won't even be onstage.

I am sitting in the classroom with a giant block of ice on the center of my desk. My imagination is completely frozen inside the ice. I can see dragon kings and talking gardens and islands made of jewels. The only way to free my imagination is to melt the block of ice. I just can't figure out how. If only I could turn into a fire-breathing dragon. But without my imagination, that's impossible. I tap my green pencil on the side of the ice. Nothing happens.

And so my paper stays blank.

CHAPTER 5

Pizza and Dog Fur (But Not Together)

Wednesday nights are Mom's book club nights. Charlie's Pizza delivers the weekly order of three pizzas at exactly 6:00 p.m. (two for us and one for book club). Between my writer's block and the library news, I am really in the dumps so I don't even run to the door when I hear the doorbell.

I've been sitting on my bed telling Abe my sad story. Abe is the best listener. He looks at me with his big, brown eyes and doesn't say a word until the entire story is finished. I know he can't really speak. But I wouldn't be surprised if he did one day. He's just that smart.

I admit I might even cry a little. Abe's fur is

a good place to stash tears when you don't want anyone to see them. I'm not ready to talk about all of this yet. It's still working its way through me, and I know sometimes if I share too early, I'm not able to hear advice. Right now, I don't want to hear lists of the things I could write about. Because I'm the one that actually has to write the poem. Mom and Dad can't write it for me. (They wouldn't anyway because they are all about us doing our own work so we understand what we are learning.)

"How can I be a famous author when I grow up if I can't even write one teeny poem in class?" I whisper. "And what if everyone gives up on the Unicorns and Macarons reading together? Will they quit our book club completely?" That almost happened once before. And it was really and truly awful.

I wrap my arms around Abe and hug tight. He is absolutely the best dog in the world. Just then, my brother Sam comes into my room. "Pizza's here," he says. "Want to watch *Cupcake Champions* with me?"

Cupcake Champions is our favorite television show. In each episode, two teams compete to bake cupcakes with all these crazy ingredients. Then the judges decide which ones are the most delicious. The winning team moves up to the next level. Eventually, there will be a final bake-off and the winning Cupcake Champions will get a lot of money for their bakery.

I shrug. I'm not really in the mood right now.

Sam waves at me to come with him. "You know I can't watch without you."

I sigh. "Fine." Abe is off the bed before I am. He gets more excited about pizza night than anyone else in the family.

The pizza is on the kitchen counter, so Sam fills his plate with five slices. I take two. Then we go into the family room. Connor is already waiting for us. He doesn't like the show as much as we do, but he watches it anyway. That's just how it is with my family. We take turns a lot.

Sam flips on the television, and the show starts. The host wears really bright-colored suits and acts super-happy to talk about cupcakes. He introduces the judges and then the teams.

We all sit on the sofa together. Abe manages to squeeze in between me and Connor. I like to tell myself he doesn't want to be too far from me since he knows that I had a tough day. But I know he's mostly here for the food.

I bite into my pizza. It's still hot and gooey. The cheese drips off the slice onto my plate. The host pulls a tablecloth off the table to reveal the special ingredients the bakers have to use in their cupcakes. "The Champion Challenge items for today are: chili flakes, mangoes, and bacon."

"Ewwwww! How will they possibly use bacon in cupcakes?" I ask Sam.

Sam squints his eyes like he's thinking about the possibilities. "It can be done. Bacon would pair nicely with chocolate. So would the chili flakes."

Chocolate and bacon? I don't think so. Now chocolate and pickles would be another story.

I see myself as a challenger on *Cupcake Champions*. I wear a bright-pink apron with my signature logo in the middle of it—a sparkling ruby. The three special ingredients I must use are: basil, cranberries, and pickles. No one has ever seen a more difficult challenge than this. But I know I can bake something scrumptious. I whip up a chocolate and pickle cupcake with cranberry and basil buttercream frosting. Then I top the cupcake with a candied pickle seed. The judges declare me the grand winner, and my cupcake goes in the Baking Hall of Fame.

The bakers start sharing their ideas for their masterpieces and mixing them up. One baker is adding chocolate, just like Sam suggested. The other team is making more of a tropical cupcake with pineapple and coconut.

Mom pops her head into the family room. "Book club is starting. Are you joining?"

I turn to Sam. "Can you tell me who wins this round?"

"You got it," he answers. "But I already know it's the chocolate cupcake."

"If you already know how it's going to turn out, then let's watch the news," Connor suggests.

"No way," Sam answers.

"I'll be right there," I tell Mom. I know from experience that a good read can fix almost anything. So I grab my notepad from my room and join Mom in the living room.

Our living room is usually set up with a large sofa and two matching chairs facing the fireplace (which we almost never use) and a low wood table in front of them. Mom keeps some special books on the table. Big books about art in Italy and castles in Ireland.

On book club nights, she moves chairs from the dining room into the living room and opens up the couch area so that there is a big ring of seating. The books on the table are replaced with a pitcher of lemonade, one large pizza, cups, plates, and napkins. Most of the group is already here. There are ten members altogether, but tonight only eight are here. Jessica's mom just joined the book club, and the other ladies are Mom's work friends.

I say hello to everyone the way Grandpa taught me. I walk around the room and look each one in the eye while shaking hands. Grandpa says a good handshake should be direct and strong. Not too wimpy, but not too grippy. Then I sit down in a chair near Mom.

"Is everyone finished with the book?" Mom asks.

Hey, that's my question! No, not really. I actually stole the question from Mom.

Everyone is finished and ready to discuss the book. Even though I haven't read it, I can learn a lot from listening. Everyone is ready with questions. Jessica's mom asks the first one, "What was your takeaway from this read?"

Mom leans over and whispers to me, "She's asking what idea stayed with each of us after finishing the book."

I write a note on my notepad, "What was your takeaway?" I like that question. I'll have to use it at our next meeting. If we ever find a book, that is.

Each person shares a thought about what they learned from the book. Even though I am in fifth grade, and Mom's book club is all grown-ups, our meetings aren't that different. (Except that their meeting won't be forced to end early because of a food fight!)

Here's what I learn:

1. The book is nonfiction (so it's a true story that really happened).
2. It's about two friends who wanted to make a difference in the world.
3. The friends began sewing special fancy quilts that they sold all over the country.
4. They took all the money they made from selling the quilts and started a school that mothers could go to for free.
5. Two of the first women to graduate from their school went on to become doctors, and two others became teachers.

It sounds like a really good book. I am going to ask Mom if I can read it too. The story of the two friends gives me an idea about me and my friends. We might be able to make a difference too.

I am sewing a quilt together. Only instead of flowers and checks, my fabric consists of all my favorite books. I am weaving the stories together. I sit in a chair sewing and sewing because my list of favorites keeps growing. The pages fit together in a pattern that creates its own story. One day, an art expert sees my work and asks to put it in a museum. My name is on a plaque above the quilt. Ruby Starr, Story Quilter.

Dad's home by the time the book club meeting is over. So we help Mom clean up the living room. I carry the cups, and Dad carries the plates.

"I saw you were busy taking lots of notes tonight," Dad tells me. He can balance all the plates in a stack on one hand. (He worked as a waiter during college.) Me, I can carry only two cups at a time, one in each hand.

"It was a good meeting," I answer. I set the cups in the sink. Then I turn to my dad. "Do you think one person can make a difference?" I run the faucet and rinse the cups. Dad sets the plates on the counter. Then he puts the rinsed cups into the dishwasher.

"I do, Ruby. In fact, that's what made me want to be a journalist. I wanted to be able to share true stories about people to inspire other people. When you hear about what is possible, it makes you believe."

Dad gives me one of the plates from the

counter. I rinse, and he keeps loading the dishwasher.

"Have you ever had writer's block?" I ask before I know the words are out of my mouth. I have a habit of speaking without thinking. I thought I didn't want to talk about the nonexistent poem, but I guess my heart wanted to talk even if my mind didn't.

Dad grins wide. "Of course! Every writer faces a blank page sometimes. Only I don't call it writer's block. I don't think a blank page means you're out of ideas. I think it means you're trying too hard, either to write something you think you should write or to write something that doesn't come from your heart. Which I guess is the same thing. When it's right, you can write."

"You used a homophone!" I notice. (Fun fact: homophones are words that sound the same but have different meanings and spellings, like horse and hoarse or right and write!) I can't help but smile. I run over to my notepad.

When it's right, you can write.

That's when I think of something. "But, Dad, how do you know when it's right?"

Dad drops a kiss on my head. "You'll know."

I'll know.

CHAPTER 6

Saving the Library: Part 1

On Thursdays, we usually have PE at the end of the day, but today Mrs. Sablinsky is showing us a film about the American Revolution after lunch. So before we even go into the classroom, she tells us to leave our backpacks on the blacktop and start running. Only no one is in a running mood on account of our wardrobe.

We are all wearing pajamas. I'm in my light-blue pajamas with pink unicorns all over them. I'm still wearing my usual green sneakers with pink Unicorn laces because even when it's Pajama Day we still have to follow the school dress code. Slippers are not allowed. Some of the teachers dressed up. But not Mrs. S. She's not a dressing-up kind of person.

Siri's pajamas are hot pink with different kinds of candy. I spot rainbow lollipops and red licorice, purple and blue jelly beans, and even yellow and white taffy. Siri and I always run together. Except that it seems strange to run around the school in my pj's (kind of like one of those nightmares where you imagine you have forgotten to get dressed in the morning). As we run side by side, I talk to Siri about the library.

"Closing the library two days a week is wrong," she says, shaking her head. I watch her ponytail swish back and forth.

"I know. No new books either." I take a big breath. "It's our library." I like to announce things in two parts. First, the introduction and second, the content. "So we're going to save it."

Siri's eyes are wide as she looks at me. "We're going to save the library? But how?"

I stretch my stride as we round the turn. Only one more lap to go.

"We're going to raise money for books. I don't know how yet. But I know the Unicorns can come up with an idea."

"Me too," Siri says as she high-fives me. It's not that easy to run and high-five at the same time, but we manage.

"Let's tell everyone now," I suggest. Siri nods. Charlotte, Daisy, and Jessica are behind us. So we slow down until they catch up. Then we walk the last lap together so we can talk.

By the time Mrs. Sablinsky calls us to go to class, we are all in agreement. Now all we have to do is figure out what we can do to raise money.

Mrs. S is all business today. First up is a spelling assignment. She hands out a list of words we have to define and then use in sentences. Whatever isn't finished will be homework. I always rush to finish if I know I can avoid homework. Less homework means more reading time for me!

After that, we have math word problems. Usually I don't like word problems, but today I realize I will really need to understand my numbers if I am going to make lots of money. I especially pay attention to the decimal point. Every penny will count if I am going to buy all those books.

Then it's time for...you guessed it! Poetry.

"Remember, tomorrow is the last day to turn in your poems. If you are late, you will not be eligible for the Poetry Read." Mrs. S is a stickler for deadlines.

While everyone is working or sharing their poems (I try not to notice most of the class is finished now, but I can't help it), Mrs. Sablinsky walks around the room.

I stare at the dreaded piece of paper.

When it's right, you can write. Dad's words

beg me not to try for something poemy, but just to write. I make a mental list of possible topics:

1. Abe (Need I say more?)
2. The American Revolution (We've been learning a lot in social studies.)
3. Food (Who wouldn't want to hear a poem about pickles?)
4. Friends (I could write one line about each friend.)
5. Family (It would be easy to write about each person I love.)

I put my pencil on the paper. Any one of these topics would be fine. I know I could write a poem worth reading out loud.

Only
nothing
happens.

That's when Mrs. Sablinsky decides to stop at my desk for a little chat.

"Sometimes students don't write anything on their paper because they aren't trying," she begins.

Uh-oh. Here we go. I'm in Trouble with a capital *T* now. There are two kinds of trouble: trouble with a lowercase *t* usually involves a lecture from my parents or teacher and a sincere apology from me, but Trouble with a capital *T* is way more serious. It usually involves a consequence of some kind.

I am just about to explain that I am trying, only nothing will come out of my pencil onto the paper, when she says this:

"Other times, I can tell people are doing their best, but something is getting in the way." Mrs. Sablinsky sighs, but not in the way she usually does when she talks to me. This sigh is more of a helpful, friendly kind of sigh. "I won't be judging the poetry but just grading you on whether you have completed the assignment. Poetry is an art form, and I don't believe you can grade an art form."

Truthfully, I hadn't even considered what grade I might get. I was more worried about how the poem would sound in front of the whole school.

"But when someone reads a poem out loud in front of the whole school, then everyone will be judging it, right?"

Mrs. Sablinsky leans down so her face is at my level. I never noticed that she has golden-brown eyes. And very long eyelashes. Longer even than Abe's. "I see what's happening now," she says quietly. "Creative writing is about writing what is inside you. Not about writing to please other people. You do that with essay writing. This is about expressing yourself. What do you want to express, Ruby?"

"I don't know," I tell her honestly. "I think of stories, and they're a lot longer than three lines with five or seven syllables. I read some poems in the library and they didn't rhyme, so I know I don't have to write something that sounds like a greeting card. I even made a list of possible subjects. Only none of them seemed just right."

"With art, there is something for everyone," Mrs. S continues. "And since you love stories, I have an idea for you. We won't be going over this in class because it's a little bit ahead of your grade level. But I think you can handle it."

Wait, is Mrs. Sablinsky really going to tell me something no one else in this entire class will know? She thinks I'm that smart?

"The first form of poetry was actually a long story poem called an epic. There are some really famous ancient epic poems. They are always about a brave hero setting out on a long journey. On the journey, the hero displays true courage."

I can't believe there is a whole kind of poetry for telling stories. I think my mouth must be hanging open in surprise. I close it quick before I embarrass myself.

"In the ancient poems, there was a special format called dactylic hexameter. It's complicated, and since you only have a day left to finish, we won't go into that now. I can teach you about it later if you want. For this assignment though, make sure you include a hero, a long journey with obstacles to overcome, and the hero returning home at the end. Do you think you would like to do that?"

So many ideas are racing through my mind on Rollerblades. *Zip-zip-zip.* I nod at Mrs. Sablinsky.

"I would most definitely," I say. She stands up to her full height again.

Suddenly, she's back to her usual self. "Will B, put the eraser down. Now! Do not put that in your mouth again!" Before she heads across the room to deal with Will B, I give her a giant grin. "Thank you," I tell her. I really and truly mean it.

I stand at the tip of a very long piece of paper. It is so long that it extends all the way from my castle into the forest. Only the bravest knight can walk across this paper and create the footprints that will tell her story. I am that knight. I dip my boots into a golden bucket of green paint. Then I begin to walk across the paper. Every step I take creates a new word. I will continue on this journey until my story is told. Generations to come will know of me and my bravery. For I am the Knight of the Epic Poem.

When the bell rings for lunch, I don't even notice. It isn't until Siri says my name that I look up from the paper. It is completely covered with words, both the front and back.

"Lunch," Siri tells me. I blink once. Twice. Then I notice that everyone is getting their lunches out of their backpacks.

I can't wait to tell Dad that when it's right, you really *can* write. I jump out of my seat. I have lots of planning to do at lunch. I can't waste a single moment. Mrs. Sablinsky is collecting the poems and putting them into two separate folders. The yellow one for incomplete. The red one for finished.

I hand her my paper. She looks down, and for a split second, I think I see her lips curve into a smile. Only it's so fast that I can't be completely sure. In case she thinks I am ready for the red folder, I tell her, "I need to work on it tomorrow. I don't have the ending yet."

She nods and slips my poem into the yellow folder. I try not to notice that I am the only one with a paper in that folder, which means I am the only student who hasn't finished yet. I just force myself to think about something else, something happier. Like chocolate-chip caramel ice cream (my favorite).

I pull my lunch bag out of my leopard backpack while Siri waits for me. Charlotte is standing near the door.

"Ready?" I ask as I hand Siri my lunch so I can pull on my sweatshirt.

But Charlotte shakes her head. "Go ahead. I'll meet you there."

"Are you sure?" Siri asks. We always walk to lunch together.

Charlotte just nods before moving toward Mrs. Sablinsky's desk. Siri and I head outside together. The weather is starting to get colder now that it's almost Thanksgiving. I have to zip up my sweatshirt one-handed while we are hurrying down the stairs. In case you haven't tried this before, it's not as easy as it sounds.

Siri and I squeeze in next to Jessica. Daisy sits across from us with Charissa, Brooke, and Sophie.

I can't wait to tell them all about my plan to save the library so we can start brainstorming ideas. But Charlotte isn't here yet. It kind of annoys me that I have something super-duper important to say but I can't say it because everyone isn't here. Instead, I take a big bite of my apple and chew really loud. Sometimes chewing really loud helps me to be less annoyed. Have you ever noticed that doing something really annoying helps you to be less annoyed about what someone else might be doing that annoys you? Which is a really long way of saying: I'm annoyed! The only thing that makes it better is that I am sitting here in my comfy unicorn pj's.

CHAPTER 7

Saving the Library: Part 2

I'm all the way around the apple once and only half listening to Charissa and Siri talking about which middle schools they are going to next year when Charlotte arrives. Or to be more exact: a giant stack of books arrives with Charlotte's pajama legs poking out underneath.

A voice comes out of the half-book, half-human body. "Mrs. Sablinsky loaned us eight copies of *Starmist*. It's not on our list, but Daisy asked for a horse story, and Sophie and Brooke wanted something under one hundred and fifty pages."

Charlotte leans forward and sets the books right in the middle of the lunch table. Now we can see her face. I haven't known Charlotte very long, but I have never once seen her light up like this. I recognize the emotion because I have experienced it myself. She's proud of herself. Charlotte Thomas has saved the day.

I flip my legs to the other side of the bench. "Thanks, Charlotte. This is really great" is what I am saying, but not what I am thinking. I wish I could say the sickish feeling in my stomach is from eating my apple too fast. But I know it isn't. I know this because I've had this problem before—and weirdly, with Charlotte. The feeling making me queasy can only be one thing:

Envy.

I am envious because Charlotte thought about asking Mrs. Sablinsky for the books. I am envious because Mrs. Sablinsky loaned them to her. And I am envious because right now everyone is jumping up and hugging Charlotte and acting like she is a hero. This was supposed to be my hero moment. Only it isn't.

"How did you get her to loan you so many books?" Jessica wants to know.

Charlotte shrugs like it was nothing. But this isn't nothing. This is one of those moments that you remember forever. "I just explained that our book club was searching for eight copies of a book we would all like, and she suggested this one. She said she has lots of copies of books in her cabinets so all we have to do is ask."

Hrumphhhhhh. As if it's that easy. I've been Mrs. Sablinsky's student for months now, and today was the first time she was actually even nice to me. It was like opposite day or something. Maybe when I get home, we'll be having breakfast for dinner.

I take the top copy of *Starmist*. The cover has a picture of a pretty gray-and-white horse running through a meadow. I like horse stories, and I've never seen this book before. Normally, I would be really excited about it (and if I'm being honest, I am a teeny bit excited). I just don't want to show it.

"What do you think, Ruby? Can we read it?" Charlotte sees me looking at the cover. I quickly put the book on the stack. If I weren't so mad right now, I might think how sweet it is that Charlotte is asking for my opinion first.

But I'm cranky. Not as cranky as a substitute we had once named Mrs. Cheer. But cranky. I shrug. "It's not up to me. We all have to agree." I look around at the rest of the Unicorns and Macarons.

"I say yes," Jessica begins.

"I say yes," Daisy continues.

"Me too," Siri adds.

Then Charissa, Brooke, and Sophie speak at the same time, "Us too."

That only leaves me—and Charlotte. "Ruby?" she asks.

I nod. "*Starmist* it is." I sit down at the table

again and open my bag of pretzels. Everyone else sits down too, except for Charlotte. She brings a copy of *Starmist* to each of us. (In lots of stories, the hero has a setback, and one of the other characters moves the story forward. It happens. But the hero is still the hero.) Pretty soon, the aide will blow the whistle, and we can get up from the table. On Thursdays, we act out plays, so my group is going to leave any minute. (Doing plays is not my favorite activity since it involves *dancing*.)

I'm running out of time. I have to make my announcement before it's too late. So I do.

"With the library closing two days a week and no new books being ordered, the library needs our help. I think we can save the library."

I offer my friends stick pretzels by holding out the open container. Everyone seems really excited to try to help.

"Does anyone have ideas about how to raise money?" I ask. I mean, a lemonade stand isn't exactly a big moneymaker. And that's probably all the experience the group here has ever had with earning money.

The ideas fly almost as fast as the corn cereal the boys are throwing at the other end of the table. Nail painting, bracelet making, babysitting, dog walking, tutoring. Then Jessica suggests a bake sale. "My sister's gymnastics team has them all the time to raise money."

Cupcakes, cookies, and books. I can't think of a more perfect combination. Everyone else agrees.

"Let's go ask Principal Snyder if we can have the bake sale at school," Siri suggests. And that's how all eight of us end up in the principal's office.

Principal Snyder is probably the nicest principal in the history of principals. He knows every single student's name in the entire school. When he walks by someone in the morning, he won't just say, "Good morning." He'll say, "Good morning, Ruby."

And when the students have a special

dress-up day, he dresses up too. Which means today, we have a meeting with our principal who is wearing pajamas!

He gets chairs for all of us, and we take turns explaining the situation.

I begin. “We know that the library hours are only Monday, Wednesday, and Friday now. Also that Mrs. Xia can’t order any new books.”

Then Jessica adds on. “The library is really important to us. So we wanted to do something to help.”

Siri speaks up. “We thought we could have a school bake sale. And donate all the money to the library.”

Daisy talks then. “Would you give us permission to have it at school?”

Charlotte finishes. “Maybe after the Poetry Read next week?”

Principal Snyder sits forward in his chair like he’s really paying attention. He looks kind of silly sitting at the desk in blue-and-brown-checked pj's. But I'm guessing we also look kind of silly sitting in the chairs in front of his desk in our pj's. Jessica is in black-and-white onesie pajamas with a hood that has two little ears on it, so she looks like a panda bear. Daisy is even wearing a robe!

"I wish all my meetings were this inspiring," he says with a smile. "I am really impressed that you all want to help the library. So not only am I giving you permission to have a bake sale, I'm also going to schedule it right now."

He stands up and walks to the door. I notice that he is wearing loafers, like my dad wears when he is in a suit. I want to giggle out loud. Loafers and pajamas definitely do not match. But you don't giggle at the principal. And you really don't giggle at the principal who has just agreed to let you save books. I let my imagination help me think of something else. Something that takes me on a journey far away.

I am about to see the Queen of Make-Believe Land to ask her if I can visit some of my friends. All the characters that have ever been created in books live in her kingdom. She sits on a throne made of twigs and tiny pink and white flowers, and she is surrounded by her court of woodland animals. I see chipmunks and rabbits and a golden fox. There is even a silver-winged owl perched on the back of her chair.

"How did you get here?" she asks. "My land is closed to outsiders."

"My imagination," I tell her.

"I have never met anyone like you," the queen says as she sends a little rabbit to bring me a map made out of fairy dust and dreams. "You are welcome here. Stay as long as you like."

My hands are still holding the map, but it has disappeared. Because I am not in Make-Believe Land. I am here in Principal Snyder's office.

He is just coming back into the room holding a piece of paper. "I have officially scheduled your bake sale for next Thursday at the Fifth Grade Poetry Read." I look at my friends and smile. I can't believe this was so easy! We are going to save the library.

He sits down at his desk again. "Now, the last thing we need to discuss. Would you like to make an announcement at the Friday morning assembly tomorrow?"

We look at one another to see if we all agree. Everyone is nodding and grinning. I am grinning the most. "How about you join me for the flag salute?" he tells us. "Then you can make your announcement."

The bell rings at just that moment. We all thank Principal Snyder and hurry to class.

All we have to do now is figure out what to bake.

The rest of the day zooms by like a spaceship flying across the galaxy. Gram picks me up, and I tell her about the bake sale right away. "Poetry and baked goods, what could be better?" Gram says as she squeezes me in a half hug. We're walking to the parking lot for Grambus.

"How about a little research trip?" Gram suggests. "We have time for a quick stop before we pick up Sam and Connor."

Gram always has the best ideas. That's how I find myself in front of a counter of cupcakes at Lizzie's Bake Shop. Lizzie's is this really cute red-and-white bakery with rows and rows of cakes, cookies, and cupcakes. They are famous for mixing ingredients into the cake part of the cupcake. You can get chocolate-chip cupcakes or strawberry cupcakes, even peanut-butter-and-jelly cupcakes.

"What should we try today?" Gram asks with a twinkle in her eye. One thing to know about Gram... She loves sweets as much as I do.

"Maybe the rainbow-sprinkle cupcake and a coconut cupcake?" I have really been wanting a coconut cupcake since Grandpa's birthday. (Especially since I never got to actually eat his birthday cake. But that's a story for another time.)

"One of each," Gram tells the man behind the counter. Then she orders five more cupcakes. Four to take home for my family and one for Grandpa.

"Just don't let George see it," I warn Gram. Abe's labradoodle brother, George, is known for making super-gigantic messes. Gram and I think he does it to get Grandpa's attention away from books. We are definitely a book-crazy family.

Gram pays, and I take our cupcakes while Gram carries the bag with the others. Then we find a little bench outside. We sit side by side on the bench.

"Ready?" Gram asks. We like to bite into our cupcakes at the exact same time.

Mmm. This might be the best cupcake ever baked. (Fun fact about me: I'm a major cupcake expert from watching so many baking shows with Sam.)

"So good," Gram mumbles. "How is yours?"

Pretty fantastic. But I take another bite to be sure. "Perfect."

"What kind of cupcakes do you want to make?" Gram asks after we switch and try each other's cupcakes. I can't tell which one I like better.

"In the cooking shows, they add unusual ingredients like lavender or red bell pepper to the batter. I was thinking about making a pickle cupcake."

"A pickle cupcake!" I can tell Gram is disgusted by the way her nose kind of scrunches and her eyes open wide. Gram and I have matching green eyes (just like my mom), and I think I might scrunch my nose that way sometimes too.

"I want to do something completely and totally Ruby."

Gram nods and then says, "A good seller finds a balance between something that is unique and something that appeals to the most people."

She's trying to tell me that a pickle cupcake might not be a big seller. But Gram doesn't know fifth graders like I do. Fifth graders *love* pickles.

"I'll take that into consideration," I say. I don't want to hurt her feelings because if I tell her she doesn't understand the tastes of ten- and eleven-year-olds, it might make her feel old. One thing I have learned about grown-ups—they do not want to be told how old they are. Not that Gram is old. She's not *old* old. She's just older than my mom, which I guess she would have to be since she is Mom's mom.

"I have loads of cookbooks, so you let me know if you need any recipes," she tells me. I finish my cupcake, and Gram takes the wrapper to the trash. Then she slips her arm around my shoulder. "Have I told you lately that you make me proud?" Gram squeezes me tight. My heart gets all melty like chocolate chips that you hold in your hand for too long. But they still taste good! "It's easy to talk about doing things. But so much harder to actually do them. You're a born leader, I tell you."

I hug Gram back. It's the best feeling to know that someone loves you as much as Gram loves me. It gives me the courage to do anything. Even dance.

And I do. I stand up and twirl around until my curls are whirling. I crash into the trash can and bump into the bench, but I don't even care. Neither does Gram.

CHAPTER 8

Not the Only Baker in Town

On Friday morning, I get to school early. My friends and I wrote out our announcement, and each of us has a different part to say. Mom has Dad take Sam and Connor to school so she can stay and watch me speak to the whole school.

Because on Friday mornings, the entire school gathers in the auditorium. Every class sits in rows with the kindergarten kids up front and the fifth graders in the back. The Unicorns and Macarons all get here early too. Every one of us is in red and white.

I am wearing a red-and-white-striped sweater with my jeans. Red and white are the school colors, and everyone is supposed to wear them on Fridays. My hair is pulled back into a ponytail because it's a little windy today. Wind and my hair are not a good combination. The wind makes it even crazier than usual, so instead of looking like a lion, I look like a lion that just woke up and forgot to brush his hair. Since no one really wants to get up in front of the whole entire school and give an announcement with lion bedhead, I went for the ponytail.

Jessica suggests that we practice once before the real thing. So we go over our lines. Jessica has the first line, and I have the last line. I've spoken at the assemblies before. But I'm not going to lie; my stomach has a few butterflies in it. They are spinning around my breakfast bagel and mixing it up with the orange juice. It makes me a little jumpy. Probably if someone tapped me on the shoulder, I would let out a little yelp. (Abe does that sometimes if we accidentally step on his tail. We would never do that on purpose, but sometimes his tail ends up in the most unexpected places.)

The morning bell rings, signaling the start of the school day. Principal Snyder steps over to us before beginning the assembly. “Everyone ready?”

We give him a thumbs-up sign. Then he turns around and picks up the microphone. “Good morning, students! Is everyone ready for a terrific Friday?”

He waits for kids to cheer.

“I see a lot of red and white today, and I’m very proud of your school spirit. Now let’s all stand for the flag salute.”

Everyone in the auditorium stands. The eight of us are already standing, so we turn to the flag and say the Pledge of Allegiance too. There’s a lot of noise in the room afterward as everyone sits down again. I never realized how loud we all sound. Maybe it’s more noticeable when you’re standing in front of everyone.

Then Principal Snyder hands us the microphone. We stand in a line in our script order so that we can pass the microphone to each other one by one as we speak.

Here is what we say:

Jessica: "We are here today to tell you about a very special fund-raiser."

Siri: "To benefit our own school library."

Daisy: "So we can have new books and a place to read them."

Charlotte: "We are having a bake sale at the Fifth Grade Poetry Read."

Charissa: "Next Thursday after school."

Brooke: "So come support our library."

Sophie: "And have a cupcake or a cookie."

Me: "Because it's all about saving books."

Everyone claps for us. Mom claps the loudest, I think. Principal Snyder gives us a wink. He looks way more principalish in his suit and tie than in his plaid pj's. I hand him the microphone, and then we take our seats. Mrs. Sablinsky even smiles at me. (With teeth!)

The rest of the assembly is short. This week we don't win the class spirit trophy. It goes to Charissa's class. Now they will get an extra recess and a Popsicle party. But it doesn't bother me because we've won before and also because I need time to work on my poem in class today. Even if there was an extra recess, I would probably have to stay in the classroom and work.

When we are dismissed, I walk with Siri and Charlotte to Room 15. At the door to the classroom, Will P is waiting for me. Today, he is wearing his red-and-white-checked socks in honor of the assembly.

"Ruby, I think it's a fantasmical idea to have a bake sale! The Polar Bears want to help bake too."

OK. This is one of those moments where someone is trying to be really nice and help me, except that I don't want his help. Only if I say that, I will sound like the most selfish, awful person. It's just that only one thought comes to mind when Will P offers to have his friends bake with us.

I imagine I am standing in front of a table loaded with trays of brownies, cookies, and cupcakes. Suddenly, pieces of cereal are showering onto the baked goods, followed by a half-eaten salami sandwich, followed by pieces of cauliflower, and a chicken leg. Then a boy runs over to the table and fake vomits right next to my signature pickle cupcakes. After that, Will B picks his nose and wipes it on one of the cupcakes. No one knows which one he touched. Every one of the customers runs away screaming. All I can do is stand there and cry.

With the tears pooling in my eyes at the thought of the horrific possibilities, I say to Will P, "I'm sorry, Will, but this is just a Unicorn and Macaron thing."

Yes, I am that selfish, horrible person. But there isn't a high demand for fake vomit and food-fight leftovers at a bake sale. Gram said I have to find the balance between unusual and appealing. And the cupcakes Will P's friends would bake are neither of those things.

Yet when Will P walks away without another word, I realize I might have just lost a friend.

And the worst part is that I deserve it.

The day kind of gets worse from there. Instead of journal time today, we have a math test and then a social studies test with an essay. Only afterward, instead of doing word searches like everyone else, I have to finish my poem.

The deadline is today. I know this because Mrs. Sablinsky has said it about ten thousand times and also because she has it written on her white board in giant red capital letters.

Only something happens to me.

I can't stop thinking about what I said to Will P. I need to focus, but I can't be creative when I am so confused inside. I know having the Polar Bears participate would be a disaster, but I also know that it really hurts to be left out.

So instead of working on my poem, I find Daisy and Jessica. Siri is a yard guard so she's helping the younger students on the playground. Usually, I would have been out there with her because I'm a yard guard too. But for a very obvious reason that starts with the letter *P* and ends with the letter *M*, I needed to stay in class.

Mrs. Sablinsky is letting everyone have free time after the tests, so she doesn't notice that I am not at my desk. I tell my friends everything. I expect them to tell me that I should go apologize to Will P right away and let his friends bake too. But they don't.

"You did the right thing," Jessica says with a definite nod.

"For sure," Daisy says. "Can you imagine what their cupcakes would look like?"

"Or taste like?" Jessica adds. "Don't even worry about it. I would have said the same exact thing."

Then why is my stomach clenching and my heart beating really superfast like I have just done a hundred sit-ups?

Just then the bell rings for lunch. *Oh no! My poem.*

If I don't finish today, it will be late. And if it's late, I can't present it at the Poetry Read. How humiliating to be selling baked goods but not even have a poem to read!

I hurry back to my desk and sit down really quickly to write. When Charlotte comes to get me,

I wave her off and tell her I will meet everyone at the lunch tables. I keep writing. But it's hard to create a brilliant ending when you are looking at the clock every single second.

Which is what I am doing.

"Ruby, time's up. I need to go to a meeting now." Mrs. Sablinsky's voice comes from far away, like I'm underwater swimming with a humpback whale, and I can barely hear her.

I keep writing.

"Ruby," she says again.

It's not done. It's not done.

"Time's up," she says again. Only this time I hear her clearly because she is standing right in front of my desk.

I look up at my teacher, hoping she will understand. "I just need a little more time. Could I stay in at lunch?" Only the students who are in trouble stay in at lunch, but right now, I fall into that category. (Definitely Trouble with a capital *T*.)

"If I didn't have a meeting, you could stay. But as it is, I am already late. I'm sorry, Ruby. But if you aren't finished, you won't be able to participate in the Poetry Read. Rules are rules."

Mrs. Sablinsky loves her rules. And I know she never breaks them. She has told us that if she breaks a rule for one person, then it isn't fair to all the others. I don't even ask her to reconsider. I already know she won't.

And that's how being mean to Will P backfires on me.

I am racing my horse down a path toward a castle. If I can deliver this important letter to the king before sundown, he will grant me my very own castle on an island surrounded by pink dolphins. I have the letter tucked into my saddle-bag. The roads are muddy, and my horse slips and almost falls down. But we race onward. Suddenly, someone steps out on the path. He wears knight's armor. Red glasses cover his eyes underneath his hood. He waves to me and asks for help. His horse has slipped and fallen in the mud. I look at the sun, dipping lower and lower in the sky. If I stop, it will be too late and I will lose my reward. I decide to ride on, passing the knight in a splash of mud. Only at that moment, the letter slips out of my bag and disappears into the puddle. When I arrive at the castle, I present myself to the king, only to find that the letter is no longer there. The king sends me away without any reward at all.

My friends want to spend all of lunch in the library looking at cookbooks. Mrs. Xia is especially touched to find out what we are doing for the library. Her eyes get misty, and then she hugs each one of us. She keeps saying we are very special girls.

I don't feel very special at this moment.

I tell my friends about the poem and how I won't be reading out loud. Daisy says she isn't reading because she doesn't like to get up in front of people. She will help me sell treats at the booth. It helps to know I won't be alone. But it still stings a little.

We're sitting on the floor near the cookbook shelf. "We need to make sure we have lots of choices," Charlotte says as we copy down recipes on index cards from Mrs. Xia.

"Maybe we can each make something different," Sophie suggests. "That way, we have eight types of sweets."

"I'd like to make brownies," Daisy says softly. "My mom has a great recipe at home."

"Then I'll do blondie bars," Jessica says. "They kind of go together." Jessica and Daisy have been besties since birth. Their moms were friends before they were born, so it was always expected that Jessica and Daisy would be a matched pair.

Siri already knows what she wants to bring. "My dad makes a signature lemon bar. It's deeeel-ish." (That's short for delicious.)

"We need to have some cookies on the table," Charissa comments. "I'll make chocolate chip or sugar cookies."

Sophie and Brooke agree to make oatmeal and snickerdoodles.

"Do you want to bake something together?" Charlotte asks me. "I was thinking of vanilla cupcakes with sprinkles."

"That's a great idea." I want to make this myself, not with my mom or Sam doing all the recipe reading. But having a friend there seems like more fun than being in the kitchen all by myself.

"I have an idea to make something really different. Pickle cupcakes!" I expect my plan to cause a great deal of excitement or even a few *Mmms*. But it falls completely flat. Worse than flat even because one person says, *Ewwwww*. I'm not sure who says it because it comes out kind of quiet. (Secret fact about me: I have super-excellent hearing. Mom says I can hear things that even Abe misses. And dogs are supposed to have superior hearing skills.)

But I love, love, love pickles. And I love, love, love cupcakes. So why not put them together?

I tilt my head to the side, brushing my ponytail off my shoulder. And say, "Well, I think they'll be a big hit. You'll see."

CHAPTER 9

Some Funny Things Aren't Really Funny at All

Weekends in the Starr family are busy. Here's how everyone spends their time on Saturday:

- Me: Practice piano. Watch two baking competitions with Sam. Read *Starmist*.
- Sam: Soccer game. Basketball practice. Baseball practice. Watch baking show with Ruby.
- Connor: Dissect an owl pellet. (An owl pellet is regurgitated, undigested food from the owl's stomach.

Can you say gross?) Read a science magazine. Practice piano.

- Mom: Wash Abe. Read a book for book club. Try a new vegan recipe made with chickpeas.
- Dad: Jog to the nearest coffee shop. Read the paper. Wash the car.
- Abe: Sleep. Eat. Repeat.

I'm lying on the sofa reading my book when Mom and Abe come into the room. Abe is still wet from his bath, and he shakes so that water droplets go flying around the room.

"Abe! I have to return this book to my teacher," I scold. I brush off the book on my sweatshirt. It's actually a story told from the horse's perspective like *Black Beauty*. I like it more than I thought I would.

"Mom, can Charlotte come over on Wednesday to bake for the bake sale?"

Mom is straightening up the room. Life with

my brothers can get messy. "Wednesday is good. I can pick you up and bring you home to bake before my book club meeting. Charlotte can stay for pizza if you are still working in the kitchen."

"Thanks," I say. Then I take a deep breath and tell her about the Poetry Unread. (This is what I am calling it now, but only to myself.)

Mom sits down next me and brushes my curls back off my face. "It's not like you to be late on an assignment."

I shrug. I don't want to tell her that I was talking with my friends instead of working. Because then she will ask me what I was talking about that was so important. And I will have to tell her about Will P. I already know what she'll say about that. Let's just say that she will not agree with my friends.

"I had writer's block," I begin. "And then it got worse. I couldn't put one line of poetry together."

Mom doesn't understand. She looks at me

like she knows there is more to the story. But she is waiting for me to tell her. "You've written poems before."

"Not ones that I was going to read in front of the whole school. I wanted to write something special." I don't know what to say now. I know I should tell her the whole truth.

Honesty is a big thing in our house. I know I should tell her. The words bubble up and try to come out. But I swallow them back when I imagine fake vomit on a cupcake tray.

"The time got away from me" is the best I can do. It's close enough to the real truth anyway.

Mom still doesn't look completely convinced. Do moms have some kind of lie detector built into their brains?

"Well, your grandparents will be disappointed, but I will let them know not to come on Thursday. I hope your bake sale isn't taking over your schoolwork."

And there it is.

She's closer to the truth than she knows. Actually, that *is* the truth. The thing is, if she already knows it without me saying it, why do I have to say it? That's what I tell myself when I say softly, "It isn't." Even though we both know it is.

Sunday after church, we stop at Gram and Grandpa's for lunch. Abe and George like to see each other for a play date at least once a week. I do wonder why Mom bothered to wash Abe before a day with George though. Because we have just climbed out of the car when George runs right through a muddy puddle and then jumps on his brother. The two dogs roll around on the grass, and then George pushes Abe into the puddle. They splash around and splatter mud all over the car, so now Dad's time was wasted as well.

Will these people ever learn?

Grandpa is waiting at the door for us. He's wearing his usual cardigan, and as always, his hair is a little messy on top like he forgot to brush it.

"How's my favorite girl?" he asks as he gives me a giant hug. "Reading anything good these days?"

Grandpa is a book person too. And we always share a little about what we are reading. He's a history professor so he reads a lot of books about American history.

"I had a social studies test on the colonies on Friday. Our essay question asked us to write a pretend letter to King George III."

Grandpa grins at me. He loves to talk history. "Tell me all about it," he says as he puts his arm around my shoulders. Then he hugs my brothers and my mom and dad.

I'm about to tell Grandpa more about my essay, but Gram runs in from the kitchen with her yellow-and-red apron tied around her waist. "Helpers! I need helpers. Pronto!" Mom and Sam and I hurry to the kitchen to help get lunch ready.

While I peel carrots, Gram asks me about the bake sale. "Still set on those pickle cupcakes, are you?"

"Absolutely!" I tell her. Peeling carrots is hard work.

Gram takes something out of the cabinet. "I got this for you." She sets a jar of pickles down in front of me. These are not the usual jarred pickles I slip into the shopping cart. These are the fancy deli kind of pickles so they are superspecial.

"Thank you!" I wrap my arms around her middle and squeeze as tight as I can. That's Gram. Even if she doesn't agree with me (because I know she doesn't think the pickle cupcakes will be very good), she still supports me.

After that, my grandma and Sam talk about colleges he likes. He's still a few years away from going to college, but Dad says it's never too early to talk about it.

We eat lunch in the dining room today. Salad and sandwiches and lots of laughter. That's life with my family. I could really enjoy it if there wasn't a little voice (OK, it might be a squeaky, nudging, not-so-little voice) telling me that I am keeping something from all of them. All of these people I love. I look around the table at my brothers, parents, and grandparents. And I know what I have to do.

So I tell them. All of it.

I begin with: "I have to tell you something that I know you won't like, but I'm telling you anyway."

I end with: "I'm sorry."

And it's not as bad as I think it's going to be.

Dad is the first one to speak. "It seems you learned a lesson about procrastinating. If you leave something until the last minute, sometimes you can't finish it. I know you wanted to read your poem out loud for all of us to hear."

"I got a little off track," I admit. But I still don't think I was wrong about Will P.

"I'm just curious. Isn't Will P your friend?" Sam asks me. "I thought you were part of his book club too."

"He is my friend. Or he was. I just said that because I didn't want to tell him the truth." It seems like I've been having a little trouble with the truth these days.

"Tell us the truth then," Mom says. I can't tell what she thinks because her voice is kind of flat. The way it is when she is disappointed. I know she remembers our talk yesterday and that now she knows that I wasn't telling her the whole story.

"They have food fights, first of all. Sometimes they even eat the food after it's all mixed up." Dad covers his mouth to keep from laughing. This is not a laughing matter. "Like tuna with grapes." I scrunch my nose. "And bitten pieces of salami." Now Grandpa is covering his mouth too.

"They throw all that food on the table?" Mom is still completely serious.

I nod. "And then they fake vomit," I begin. Connor snorts out a laugh and then covers his mouth. "But they pretend it's real." I notice Sam is shaking from keeping his laughter inside. "Right on the lunch table."

Now even Mom and Gram can't hide the smiles.

"That was very specific," Mom comments.

Then all at once, the entire room bursts out laughing. No one can stop. Grandpa is dabbing his eyes with his napkin. Gram is holding her stomach. And Connor is falling out of his chair.

The only one not laughing—

Is me.

Because some funny things aren't really funny at all.

Later, after we get home, my parents come to my room and I get a "talk." I don't really want to dwell on the details. Let's just say they remind me that being a good friend means putting the other person first. And that excluding Will was wrong, especially since he was there for me when I really needed a friend. Apparently, loyalty means sticking by someone no matter what, even if his friends fake vomit on the table. The worst part is that my mom and dad are right.

If Will had done the same thing to me, I would have been really hurt. Sometimes it helps to imagine being the person on the other side. At least it does for me. Things look really different when you flip them around.

Me: It's just a Unicorn and Macaron thing. Will: [Silent walk away]

Will: It's just a Polar Bear thing. Me: [Silent walk away]

Definitely different.

Monday morning comes faster than I would have liked. I'm not a Monday person anyway, but this Monday is trying my patience. I might have to remove Mondays from my week altogether.

First, it's clear when I say hello to Will P that he is giving me the Shun. Someone would only recognize the Shun for two reasons:

1. You have received the Shun before.
2. You have given someone the Shun. (And that's even worse.)

I'm sorry to say that I fit in the second category. It wasn't my best moment. The Shun is when you pretend someone doesn't exist. You act like they are totally invisible. That's what Will does to me. Let me explain that receiving the Shun is as bad as it sounds.

Next, Mrs. S has a printed list for the order

in which our class will be reading their poems. Everyone but me and Daisy is reading. Even Will B is reading. For some reason, that makes me even more depressed.

At lunch, I barely taste my carrot muffin and celery sticks. Mom usually sends me the same lunches so when I get a different one, it's like a silent message from her. It's code for *I love you* and *I'm thinking of you*. Sometimes it really helps. Today, not so much. Even when you know why someone is giving you the Shun, and even when you know you sort of maybe deserve it a little, it still makes your stomach hurt.

Then my friends want to practice their poems. One more reminder of the disaster I have made for myself. Daisy and I sit on the field and listen as each one reads her poem. I have to admit, they are impressive. I have some pretty creative friends.

Siri has managed to find information about the Statue of Liberty without making the poem seem like a history lesson. Charlotte has written a poem all about reading and books. To someone like me who knows what Charlotte was like when she first came here, it's an awesome moment.

Jessica has written a haiku about horses. She has even written a second one about dogs. I like the horse one a little better (but don't tell her 'cause I say I love them both). Daisy is happy to listen because she chose not to speak. I didn't choose not to speak. I just messed up and lost my chance. So it's different for me.

I mope through the rest of the day trying not to notice that Will P talks to everyone else except me. By the time Mom picks me up, I am exhausted. All I can think about is climbing in bed with my stuffed white rabbit. (I've had him since I was two.) Mom and I had planned to run to the grocery store to get all the ingredients for when

Charlotte comes over on Wednesday. Even though it should be fun to pick out frosting and sprinkles and cute cupcake wrappers, it's kind of not fun. I pretend it is for Mom because she's taking time to help me and buy all these groceries. But I'm like a doughnut.

CHAPTER 10

Sprinkles and a Shun Are a Recipe for Disaster (with a Capital *D*)

Tuesday isn't much better than Monday, even though it's Book Club Tuesday. Except that we cancel the meeting because we have to make signs for the bake sale. So it's not even like Book Club Tuesday at all.

Making the signs seems like fun at first. We get to go into the auditorium and draw on poster boards. I have just finished drawing tiny books with wings and writing SAVE THE LIBRARY in giant bubble letters when Will P and the Polar Bears come into the room with Principal Snyder.

I wish I could fly away with my own wings.

I am sitting in the auditorium. Suddenly, Will P and the Polar Bears walk in. I unfurl my giant golden wings and take off into the sky. I fly in formation with the tiny books with wings from my poster. We travel over mountains, across valleys, and through jungles. We drop rolled pages of our stories like presents all over the world for people to read. We share the gift of words with everyone.

Only I'm not flying over mountains. I am stuck here in school, and now I am trapped. Why would Will P be here? And with the principal. Am I in Trouble?

Then this happens:

"Girls, you have some helpers with your bake sale. Will and Bryden came to me and asked to help raise money with you. I think it's wonderful to have so many students who want to give back. I have suggested they set up a separate table and manage their own baked goods. The more, the merrier."

It might be OK if I hadn't said what I said to Will. It also might be OK if he wasn't still giving me the Shun. But he is. I can tell from the way he says hello to all the other girls but not me. Then he asks Siri to pass him a poster board even though the pile is closest to me.

That's when I get mad. Not steam-coming-out-of-my-ears mad like a cartoon character.

Just pinching my mouth into a straight line and scrunching my eyes mad. If he thinks his gross cupcakes will make more money than our delicious ones, then he isn't as smart as I thought he was.

I'd like to say the worst part of the day is over. But I can't. Because after lunch is the poetry rehearsal. And I have to sit in a chair and watch every single fifth grader read a poem. Correction: every single fifth grader except for me and Daisy. Even Jason is up there on stage completely awake. And guess what? His haiku about the sky is one of the best poems.

Wednesday isn't much better. It's dress rehearsal day. Did I mention that special clothes are required for this event? Everyone is asked to wear black pants or skirts and white tops. The teachers want it to be really formal. Did I mention I messed up and I'm not participating?

I droop through lunch and count the minutes until the day will be over. When Mom picks me and Charlotte up after school, I am so happy I could sing a little song about pickle cupcakes.

Mom has apples and peanut butter already waiting on two plates in the kitchen. After we eat, we are ready to get to work.

"I've cleared the afternoon so I can help you girls bake. Gram is picking up Sam and Connor, and I am all yours," Mom tells us with a big smile. She is wearing her stay-at-home clothes—a flowy white shirt and cuffed jeans.

Maybe it's the Poetry Unread. Maybe it's something else. But I am a little prickly. I'm a bear that missed its hibernation day. So this is what I say to my mom:

"Actually, we want to do this on our own."

I try not to notice the look on Mom's face at that moment. It makes something in my heart twinge, almost like it has skipped a beat. But she doesn't argue. She just pastes a smile on her face that I know isn't her real smile and sets out the bowls and baking trays. Then she leaves us alone. I flip on the old radio and play some oldies. I'm determined to make this special.

"Let's make the same batter for both cupcakes. Then we can separate it, and I will add my pickles."

"I've never baked from scratch before," Charlotte tells me. She pulls her hair back into a ponytail and washes her hands at the sink. "I'm ready!"

I take out Mom's cookbook, and we follow along with the recipe. Except that baking is easier with Mom and Sam. Because Charlotte and I make a little teeny bit of a mess.

"We need two cups of flour," I say as I open the bag of flour and try to pour it into the measuring cup. Somehow, more flour lands on the counter than in the cup. I use a butter knife to level off the top of the measuring cup.

"Looks good," Charlotte says as she dumps the flour into a bowl. She checks the recipe. "Next, one half teaspoon of salt."

The salt container is way bigger than the little teeny one half teaspoon. So when she pours out the salt, it spills over the sides and onto the floor. Now Charlotte and I are slip-sliding around the kitchen.

"My brother showed me how to crack an egg into a bowl with only one hand," I share. "He says it's all in the flick of the wrist." It's true that Sam can crack an egg with one hand just like the chefs on television. I've never tried it though. Until now.

I hold an egg against the side of the mixing bowl. *Tap. Tap.*

Nothing happens. I barely see a little scratch in the surface of the shell. I'm not sure how to break an egg and flick my wrist at the same time.

"Maybe you need to hit it harder," Charlotte suggests.

So I tap a bit harder. Now there is a small crack on the side of the shell. But it's not cracked enough to split in half.

"Go ahead," she encourages.

So I do. I smash the egg against the edge of the bowl and twist my hand around at the same time. Only instead of splitting the shell neatly into two sides so that the egg drops into the bowl, I end up crunching the shell into tiny pieces and exploding the insides of the egg all over my hand and even dripping some down my arm.

"Let me try," Charlotte suggests. She can't get the egg to break at all.

"We need to make sure we have two eggs in the batter," I tell her. So I crack the egg using two hands. This time I get most of it in the bowl, so we move on to the butter and sugar. That part goes a little bit better. The sugar is easy to pour, and the butter only has to be unwrapped.

I check the recipe once more. I'm like a

Cupcake Champion already. “A little milk, and then we are ready to go,” I announce. Charlotte pours, and I measure. Guess what? We get it exactly right!

We put the bowl underneath the mixer and turn it on. This I already know how to do.

“Did you put in the baking powder?” I can’t remember if I did or she did. The recipe says one half teaspoon. We need to make sure we have all the ingredients in the mixture. Mom says baking is very precise.

She has a smear of flour across her nose. “I think so.”

So Charlotte and I put the pink wrappers into the cupcake pans. Then we take turns pouring the batter into them.

I pull out the jar of pickles from Gram. First, I do a taste test. (What? I have to make sure these are top-quality pickles.) I cut one in half, and Charlotte and I each take a piece.

Yum! Super-salty and delicious.

I'm not sure how to add these to the batter since we have already scooped it into the cups. I decide to cut slices and then cut the slices in half again. I drop three of each into the cupcake batter in my tray. "This should work," I say with a grin.

"I'm going to leave mine plain," Charlotte decides. "Then I can jazz them up with decorations."

"I think that will be most excellent," I say in my fake British accent.

That's when Mom comes into the kitchen. Her eyes get really big when she sees the mess. "Wow, this is some project."

"Sorry, Mom. We got a little carried away. We'll clean it all up." I plan to eat three more pickles and then start cleaning.

"Good idea." She peeks into our trays of cupcakes. "Looks like you're ready for the oven." Mom doesn't like me to use the oven by myself.

That's why she watches while I slide the trays onto the rack and close the door.

I set the timer for sixteen minutes.

Sixteen minutes whiz by when you are cleaning up a really big mess in the kitchen. Before we have even finished the counter, the timer beeps. I am so excited to see our work.

"Mom!" I call. When she doesn't come immediately, I run into the living room to get her. "The oven beeped. I need you."

She sets down her book and follows me back into the kitchen. Charlotte and I stand side by side as Mom opens the oven door.

"Oh no!" I can hardly believe what I am seeing.

Something has gone wrong.

Very, very wrong.

Mom puts on her yellow daisy oven mitts and takes out the trays. When she sets them on the counter to cool, we take a closer look. Charlotte's cupcakes are way too big. They have overflowed onto the tray. They don't even look like cupcakes at all. More like blobs of cake.

My cupcakes are worse. Worser even (if that was a word). They are a Disaster with a capital *D*.

Because my cupcakes are shrimpy little cakes that look runny and greenish. They are the exact opposite of appetizing. In fact, they look like something you would find underneath Will B's desk. (Need I say more?)

The only person to blame for this Disaster is me. It isn't Charlotte's fault. Because she came over to bake with me and my mom, even though she could have baked with her grandma at home. My attitude ruined her cupcakes too.

I turn to my friend. "I'm so sorry, Charlotte. I know the cupcakes would have been perfect if I had let my mom help. I wanted to do it by myself, and that wasn't fair to you." My apologies are getting a lot of practice lately. I can tell they are getting better.

"It's not your fault, Ruby. We both got confused about the recipe." Charlotte gives me a little hug.

But I have another apology to make. More practice.

"I'm sorry, Mom. I shouldn't have treated you like that. Could you help us?" I try to make my best puppy-dog sad face. It gets Mom every time.

"Of course I'll help you," she says as she touches her finger to the tip of my nose. When she does that, I know everything is going to be all right. Maybe even better than all right. "All you had to do was ask."

"Let's get rid of these," she says as she picks up the tray of pickle cupcakes. "Unless you want to try one?"

Charlotte and I call out at the same time. "No way!"

The second round of cupcakes is much better than the first. I have still insisted on my pickle cupcakes. Mom gets me to chop up the pickles into tiny pieces, and the liquid doesn't mess up the recipe. She encourages Charlotte to add sprinkles to her batter so the cupcakes have confetti pieces in them after they bake.

Then we make frosting. I add some green food coloring to mine to keep with the pickle theme. Charlotte likes hers in plain white so the sprinkles really show. We both decide not to try our cupcakes until tomorrow at the bake sale. I want my tasting to be a big reveal like on *Cupcake Champions*.

When the doorbell rings at 6:00 p.m. with the three pizzas from Charlie's, I'm exhausted. I never knew saving a library could be this much work.

In the morning, Mom helps me bring the cupcakes to school in plastic containers. We leave them in the office because the Poetry Read isn't until after school.

"I'll see you at home tonight," Mom says as she kisses me good-bye. She's wearing her officey clothes, a black shirt and gray pants. Gram is picking me up today since Mom has to go to work.

I hold on to her a little tighter than usual. I know I'm ten, but sometimes a girl just needs her mom. This is one of those moments. Mom seems to understand even without me saying it because she kisses the top of my head and whispers, "You know how to fix this. I believe in you." I hug her one more time and consider following her out the door and hiding in the trunk of the car. Except that I'm not sure I could breathe in there. And also, how would I eat lunch? I'm a big believer in the importance of good nutrition. Without it, your brain just doesn't seem to work right. At least mine doesn't.

I'm not supposed to go to the classroom today. It's a completely mixed-up sort of day. Because I have to go to straight to a field trip. Well, it's not a real field trip because we don't actually leave school. We stay at school, and the field trip comes to us, which makes it a field trip that isn't really a field trip.

I meet my friends in front of the auditorium. They are all wearing their fancy black-and-white poetry clothes. Mrs. Sablinsky said we should line up here today and leave our backpacks outside. "Do you know what we're doing?" Siri asks.

I shake my head. "No idea."

"I hope it's about animals," Jessica says. "I heard there's one field trip where they bring an actual wolf to the school."

"A real wolf?" Charlotte's eyes are big at that thought.

I'd like to meet a wolf in person. I've met a lot of them in books, and they are usually the bad guys. I'm guessing they are different when you meet them on a leash at your school.

Mrs. Sablinsky arrives just then. “Here we are,” she says. “Students, follow me.” We all smoosh behind our teacher and walk through the door to the auditorium.

Right away, I know what we are doing. We are taking a trip around the world.

Because there is a giant map covering the floor.

“Everyone, please take off your shoes so you can walk on the map,” Mrs. Sablinsky tells us. Take off our shoes? Really?

(Fact about me: I am not a big fan of taking off my shoes in public because:

1. Sometimes feet can smell. Hey, it happens to all of us. Only this would be super-embarrassing at school.
2. Occasionally I wear socks that do not match. I don’t do this on purpose. But sometimes I grab the first two socks I can find in the drawer. Many

> times they are not matching, which
> is also potentially embarrassing.)

Today I am wearing mismatched socks. It's true. I have on one pink tie-dyed sock and one sock that has a pig on it. Except that the pig looks like a cross between a pig and a cow. In case you have never seen a pig crossed with a cow, let me tell you, it's not cute at all. Not even a little bit. I wonder where I got these socks in the first place.

Mrs. S hands out papers with the same map printed on it. She also passes out pencils. "I will be calling off numbers to pair you up. Then you can walk around the map and try to locate all the places marked on the floor."

Oh no. It's the worst when teachers count off numbers like one, two, three, four, five. Then they start over: one, two, three, four, five. After that, they tell the ones to pair up. And the twos to pair up. You get the idea.

Only we thought we would get to pair up with a friend standing next to us so we have lined up with our chosen partners. So I'm next to Siri. That's when the teacher pulls a switcheroo, and there is no possible way that the person standing next to you will be your partner. Which is a very long way of saying…I get partnered with Will P!

Will is wearing black-and-white socks with dominos on them (his match) and a white shirt with black pants (no shorts!). Also, he is wearing a frown.

"I like your socks," I tell him. No response.

"What kind of cupcakes did you bake?" No response.

Will is taking this Shun very seriously. I'm thinking that's because he is really mad at me, maybe even never-be-friends-again mad. I try to hide my socks from view. But now we have to walk across the map and try to locate different places. Every time Will looks down, I move my foot back so that the pig is hiding behind my other sock. It's not easy to balance on one leg. This must be what it's like to be a flamingo.

I am not me. I am a flamingo with mismatched socks. All the other flamingos are wearing striped socks and polka-dot socks that actually go together. When no one is looking, I take off one of the socks while still balancing on one leg and throw it into the lake. A frog hopping by brings the sock back to me. Now everyone knows it is mine.

I know what I have to do. I'm getting better with practice, but it's hard to apologize to someone who won't even look at you. Plus, everyone in class would hear me. That would be super-duper embarrassing, even worse than wearing one weird pig-cow sock.

When the field trip that isn't really a field trip is finally over, I breathe a sigh of relief. Maybe I can say sorry later. Or maybe a dragon will come and carry me away to an island where friends never get mad and everyone has matching socks.

CHAPTER 11

Polar Bears Can Bake

Setting up for the bake sale is one of the highlights of my fifth-grade year. We have our own table in the back of the auditorium, and our posters are taped all around to advertise.

My poster is right in the middle of the table. One of the office ladies brings us an actual cashbox. It's gray metal and has some dollars and quarters inside to make change. Mrs. Xia comes by to help. She suggests we charge one dollar for all items. Everyone agrees that this is a good price.

When I open my box of cupcakes and set them on the table, I think they look pretty delicious. Charlotte's look even better. If I'm being honest, green isn't the most appetizing frosting color.

Siri's lemon bars are more like triangles than squares. "I had a little trouble getting them out of the pan," she explains.

Jessica and Daisy have their blondie bars and brownies plated together in two circles. They look like bestie treats. "I can't wait to try one of each," I tell them. Mom has given me money to buy treats and to donate to the cause.

Charissa, Brooke, and Sophie's cookies look like they are from a real bakery. I know they will be big sellers. "Yours look professional!" I say with a smile.

The smile stays on my face all the way until I see the other bake sale set up across from ours. The Polar Bears have a real red-and-white tablecloth and little stands for all the cupcakes. I move closer to be sure. Yep, it looks like a finale for a baking competition. Now I know why Mrs. Sablinsky makes us do projects in class. There is no way Will and his friends made all these cupcakes. I can't believe they even helped make these cupcakes. They have perfect swirly frosting and real candy flowers.

Will P is arranging napkins in a flower shape. I realize that maybe he did bake some of these himself. Maybe he likes cooking as much as my brother Sam does. Somehow that makes what I did even worse. Before I even think about it, I am walking right up to his booth.

"Will, your booth is stupendiferous! It's even wondermazing." The Will P signature word mash-up gets him to look at me. But I don't stop there. "I am so sorry for what I said. I didn't mean it. Not even a little bit. It wasn't about you, not really. It was more about your friends. Sometimes they mess up our book club meetings with their food fights." I sigh. "I really don't like salami."

Will's frown completely disappears by that last part. He grins at me. "I really don't like salami either! I just wanted to help the library too. I didn't want to be in a fight with you."

I smile at him. "Me neither."

"Friends?" he asks.

"Friends." I answer. "Did you really bake these?"

Will nods. "Baking is one of my talents." I look at the cupcakes close up. They are fancier than the ones at Lizzie's Bake Shop.

"Mine can't even come close to yours. Only did you make any with pickles?"

Will scrunches up his nose like he smells something awful. "Absolutomundo not. Did you?"

I can't help but giggle as I say, "Absolutomundo yes!" Then, "Now let's sell some cupcakes!"

I am not at the bake sale anymore. I am in an empty white room with three doors. There are a red door, a blue door, and a green door. I open the green door. Outside is a gigantic mountain of shiny slime. In my hand, I hold my envy. It's gooey and sticky and clings to anything it touches. I drop it onto the mountain and close the door. Now it will stay where it belongs.

Then it's time for the Poetry Read. Only, instead of being mad that I'm not up there reading my poem, I actually listen to everyone else. Their poems are funny and sad and even silly. I realize that Mrs. Sablinsky was right (I know, I can't believe I am thinking this either!), and that it was the getting up in front of everyone that was holding me back and not the actual writing. It sort of makes sense now. I was getting in my own way. Next time I need to

let
    myself
        just
            be
                me.

Daisy and I sit in chairs at our booth and watch from the back of the auditorium so we have a really good view. At the end, I am pretty sure I clap even louder than the parents. The minute the show is over, all the students and parents get up from their chairs. And then come to our booths!

Mrs. Xia is our very first customer.

"I've been a librarian for twenty-five years," she tells us. "You are the most wonderful students I have ever had." Then she buys a brownie and three cookies. The other girls have joined Daisy and me so we have plenty of help.

"The Macarons can take the payments if the Unicorns hand people their cookies and cupcakes," Charissa offers.

"That sounds like a good plan," Siri answers. We all agree. So Siri and Jessica hand Mrs. Xia her baked goods, and Charissa puts the money into the metal box.

Mrs. Sablinsky is second in line.

"This is a very impressive table," she tells us. "What kind of cupcakes are those?" she asks us as she points to my greener-than-green masterpieces.

"Ruby made pickle cupcakes," Charlotte tells her.

Mrs. Sablinsky nods as if this isn't unusual at all. Then she says the most unbelievable thing ever: "I absolutely love pickles! I'll buy one of those."

Now I know that I made a really big deal out of these cupcakes. And I've told all the doubters that these cupcakes will be fabulous. But I haven't actually tasted one. So watching my teacher prepare to eat my cupcake sends fear shivering down my neck all the way to my pig-cow sock. The other girls are selling to everyone in line, but I am not moving. I am not even sure I am breathing as I watch Mrs. Sablinsky open her mouth and bite into the green cupcake. I press my lips together as I watch her chew.

And then it happens. I see my teacher smile. It's a smile I have never seen on her face before. It's a stupendous best-day-ever kind of smile.

In that moment, I realize the craziest thing I have ever realized in my life: Mrs. Sablinsky is a little bit like me. She really is. I will never, ever look at her the same again. Because someone who would eat a pickle cupcake and like it just might be the kind of person who would invite a talking chipmunk to tea. And that changes everything.

After that, time zooms by like dragonflies as we sell cupcakes, cookies, and brownies to parents and teachers and lots of students.

"I'd like to try a pickle cupcake, please," my next customer says. Only it isn't just any customer. It's my dad. I am so happy to see him that I run around the booth and hug him tight.

"Thanks for coming," I tell him. It means a lot that he is here, even though I didn't get to read my poem.

"I have a surprise for you," he says with a wink. "I thought a little publicity might help your bake sale and the library."

Dad points behind him to a camera from the news station. There is even a reporter with them. "I'm running a story on your mission to save books."

I am so excited I can't speak. And that's really unusual for me. A little tear even squeezes out of my eye. (Ruby Starr Exception to the No Crying at School Rule: Happy tears are acceptable as long as they are limited to one or two tears in total.)

Dad introduces us to the reporter. Her name is Holly Day. She's super-pretty and is wearing a fancy blue suit and high heels.

Holly turns to the camera and says: "Today I am with a group of extraordinary fifth-grade students who want to make a difference. They have started a fund to save books. That's right. These students are raising money for their school library. They also have their own book clubs. Let's introduce them, shall we?"

Then Holly asks all of us to say our first names. Mine sounds like this: "I'm Ruby."

Next, she has the cameraman film our bake sale tables and the crowd. It's pretty exciting to think that I'm on the news, even if it isn't my best hair day.

Then Holly asks me a question. "Ruby, I heard that you started this whole thing with your book club. Can you tell me a little bit about how that came about?"

I know I was so nervous about reading my poem in front of the school that it gave me a freezing writer's block. But when I'm talking on camera, I'm not nervous at all. I guess you could say that I'm a natural. Plus, it helps that I'm talking about my favorite thing—books.

"Well, first, I love books and reading. And then my mom had a book club so it made me think about starting one of my own. So I did, with my friends." I point to Siri and Jessica and Daisy and Charlotte. "And then I invited other people at school to join us, and they started their own book clubs. That's kind of the short version. The long version would take a while to tell." I finish the last part with a grin at my dad. He gives me a thumbs-up.

"Can you tell us why you are raising money today?"

"I need a little help to answer this question because I didn't do this by myself." I wave my friends over to help me with this part, even Will and his friends. When everyone is all together, I continue. "Our library doesn't have enough copies for the book clubs. Also, they have cut down the days the library is open. So we thought maybe we could do something to help."

Holly turns to the camera now. "It's wonderful to see so many students excited about reading. So before we close, why don't you tell us your favorite books?"

Then she goes down the line asking the Macarons, the Polar Bears, and the Unicorns what their favorite books are. I hear lots of titles I recognize and love. I'm at the end of the line so I have time to think. Except I don't have a favorite book because I love them all. So that's what I say. "My favorite is usually the book I am currently reading."

At the end, Holly tells viewers where they can send donations to our library. We thank her and then go to clean up. That's when I realize that I still haven't tried one of my own cupcake creations. Lucky for me, there's still one left. So I put a dollar in the box. Then I pick up the green cupcake and take a giant bite.

I know it's going to be amazing. I expect it to be delicious.

But I never imagined it would be this fabulous! It is:

The. Best. Cupcake. Ever!

After that, we sit in a circle on the floor and count up all the money in the metal boxes. Here is the final count: The Polar Bears, $149, and the Unicorns-Macarons, $101! That's enough money for a bunch of new books. Maybe even eight copies of *The Misfit Girls*.

On the way home, Dad tells me something super-exciting. People who saw us on the news have started sending in donations for the library, so we will have enough funds to keep the library open all week long—and buy some new books! He also tells me he's proud of me. And that's the best thing of all.

But there is still one thing I have to do. On Sunday afternoon, I invite my family to hear my first ever epic poem. Maybe I didn't get to read in front of the entire school, but the people that matter most to me are here: Mom, Dad, Sam, Connor, Gram,

Grandpa, and of course the dogs, Abe and George. Everyone sits on the sofa and chairs in my grandparents' living room and waits for me to read my poem out loud.

I clear my throat. "Thank you for being here. My epic poem is called 'Searching for the Lost Book.'" Then I begin reading the words on the page. Only I forget I am reading and instead imagine myself in the poem. Here it is:

Searching for the Lost Book

BY RUBY J. STARR

From a kingdom called Melonia, a call was heard
far and wide
For the bravest knights to find the lost book
It had been stolen from the king's treasure chest
And no one had seen it for a hundred years
Though many knights had searched through the land
None succeeded in finding it

Until a knight named Star arrived in the court
Though she was smaller than the other knights
And younger too
She had a secret skill that was hers alone
Imagination
With it, she could see what others could not
And succeed where others had failed
Star crossed the driest deserts where windstorms pushed and pulled
She climbed the highest snowy peaks where only hawks dared to go
She swam to the deepest oceans where sunken ships lay buried below
Until she reached a library as large as a castle and filled with books of all kinds
And readers young and old
There she found the lost book on a shelf with many others
And she understood that this is where it belonged
In a place where it could be found and read over and over again

Instead of locked away in a chest
The brave knight had traveled the world but had never
known a home
Until she entered this library and met readers just like
herself
So she never returned to the kingdom of Melonia
Instead, she stayed with the Lost Book
In the Library of the Found

I am Star the Knight in the Library of the Found. My journey isn't over; instead it's only beginning. For I am surrounded by hundreds of books and lots of readers just like me.

My family claps for me. I take a little bow, and then I can't help myself—I have to twirl around once. It's not the danciest of moves, but sometimes a spin is just the thing. Because I did it! I saved the library, and I wrote a real poem. I even managed to get an A although my poem was late.

At the end of every good story, the hero learns something about herself. I realized that my favorite characters didn't save the world by themselves. I couldn't have written the poem or saved the library alone either. I needed my family and the Unicorns and the Macarons and the Polar Bears, plus Mrs. Xia and Mrs. Sablinsky and Principal Snyder. Hey, I guess this is how those award speeches always get so long. Wait a second. I almost forget Abe and his extraordinary listening skills. I guess what I'm saying is that in order to do something really fabulous, it takes a lot of help.

Always remember: when friends read together, anything is possible!

Acknowledgments

Thank you for reading this book. I hope you enjoyed Ruby's latest adventure!

Many people have helped make this book possible so I want to say thank you because this is a dream come true for me.

Thank you to my dynamic agent Stacey Glick for being a kindred spirit, for your friendship, and for always believing in my work. My team at Sourcebooks Jabberwocky is incredible, and I am grateful to all of you for working so hard on this series. Annie Berger, my brilliant editor, many thanks for your guidance and support and for every time you laughed at one of Ruby's jokes. Every page is better because of you. Elizabeth Boyer, thank you for making the manuscript look so good and for telling me every last-minute change was still possible! Sarah Kasman, thanks so much for your sunny emails and for all your work on the manuscript. Diane Dannenfeldt, thank you for combing through the manuscript and making it perfectly perfect. Nicole Hower, thank you for creating Ruby's beautiful signature design, and then surpassing it with this book! Jeanine Murch, thank you for seeing inside my imagination to bring Ruby's world to the page. I am so blessed to be working with you. Katy Lynch, who has worked so hard to make sure readers meet Ruby, thank you for every email and phone call. Your counsel has been invaluable to me. Alex Yeadon, who makes even the impossible event possible somehow through her magic. I have no idea how you do it, but thank you! Steve Geck, Todd Stocke, and Dominique Raccah, thank you for making me part of the Sourcebooks family. I couldn't imagine a better home for Ruby.

To Aubrey Poole, thank you for taking a chance on Ruby. I will forever be indebted to you.

To my friends, old and new, who have come to book signings and shared Ruby with their kids and neighbors, hugs to you. To my family, you are the best cheering team ever, and I can't thank you enough for your enthusiastic support and your prayers. To my daughters, Ava and Caroline, this book is as much yours as mine. Thank you for reading every revision and for being with me every step of the way. And my deepest thanks to God for the many blessings I have received.

Don't miss Ruby's other adventures!

About the Author

Deborah Lytton writes books for middle grade and young adult readers. She is the author of *Jane in Bloom* and *Silence*. Deborah has a history degree from UCLA and a law degree from Pepperdine University. She lives in Los Angeles, California, with her two daughters and their dog, Faith. For more information about Deborah, visit deborahlytton.com.